DATE DUE			

**F
HAL**

Hall, Lynn.

Zelda strikes again!

**LAKESHORE ELEMENTARY SCHOOL
HOLLAND, MI   49424**

Zelda Strikes Again!

Also by Lynn Hall

Lynn Hall

Zelda Strikes Again!

Harcourt Brace Jovanovich, Publishers
San Diego   New York   London

Z17029   8-93

Library of Congress Cataloging-in-Publication Data
Hall, Lynn.
Zelda strikes again!
Summary: Five more episodes in the zany life of
Zelda Hammersmith, in which she crashes a stranger's
funeral, sneaks on board an airplane, causes her
substitute teacher to collapse, and gets in all kinds
of trouble.
[1. Humorous stories] I. Title.
PZ7.H1458Ze 1988 [Fic] 88-2194
ISBN 0-15-299966-3

Designed by Nancy J. Ponichtera
Printed in the United States of America
First edition

A B C D E

Contents

Zelda Strikes Again!

1. Zelda at the Pearly Gates

My name is Zelda Hammersmith. Maybe you've heard of me. If you have, it's probably because of my reputation. I have a bad reputation for getting into trouble, but it's not my fault.

Usually.

Sometimes.

Well, okay, it's usually my fault, but my heart is in the right place. At least that's what my mom says. I live with my mom in Perfect Paradise Trailer Park, on the edge of town.

The last time I got into trouble, it definitely wasn't my fault. It was Cindy's fault.

Cindy is my mom's best friend. At least she tells everybody she is Mom's best friend, and that makes me mad, because she's not. I am. In fact I don't see why Mom needs any friends besides me. I'm cute and lovable . . . and handy. She doesn't even have to call anybody to say "Come over, I feel like visiting." I'm already there.

So that's one reason I don't like Cindy. The other reason is that she's silly. I don't care if she *is* twenty years older than I am, and it's not nice to say an old person is silly, but she is. She's always talking about her boyfriends, and how they're always wanting to marry her. She lies. Nobody could want to marry a person who wears so much perfume so early in the morning.

She was over at our trailer Saturday morning, right after breakfast. Wearing high heels with her slacks. And perfume, of course. And a blouse that looked like tiger skin. That was probably supposed to look sexy, but I thought it looked silly.

So did her makeup. Can you imagine gluing on fake eyelashes—for a Saturday morning? They were so heavy she had to hold her head back to see out from under them. She looked like she had caterpillars on her eyes.

She and Mom sat at the table and drank coffee and smoked cigarettes and talked lady talk. Mom looked like she was supposed to look at nine o'clock on a Saturday morning. She wore her striped nightshirt with the prisoner number across the chest, and she had bare feet and messy hair.

I shoved onto Mom's chair and made her put her arm around me while they talked. It was boring talk, and I'd rather have been outside doing something, but I felt like I had to claim my territory. Mom was my territory.

So I leaned on Mom and pulled her arm hairs and listened to silly old Cindy.

She was talking about some guy at the restaurant last night who wanted to marry her. She works as a hostess at the Sirloin and Brew because of all the men she gets to meet there.

At the end of this long, boring story that I didn't believe anyway, she said, "Come on, Ruth. Get dressed. Let's go over to the laundromat and look for divorced guys."

"I'm not interested in looking for divorced guys. I'm still legally married, don't forget."

"Fat lot of good that does you, with him off in Nashville trying to be a country and western music star, and you here. You've got to live, woman. Get rid of the deadweight and find yourself a live one."

I pulled harder on Mom's arm hairs and made her yelp. "Knock it off, Zelda. You want a bald-armed mother, or what? Why don't you go clean your room?"

Go clean your room. Go clean your

room. The four ugliest words in the English language. I pushed off from Mom's chair and went down the hall like I was going to my room, but I stopped by the water heater. I leaned against the wall, where they couldn't see me and listened in on them. Served them right. Besides, it's a fact of nature that grown-ups only talk about the good stuff when there are no kids in the room.

"Listen," Cindy said, "I've got tonight off. Let's you and me get duded up and go have some fun. Come on. Get a sitter for the kid. You need a night out on the town."

"Nah. Thanks anyway, but I better pass. I'm kind of sticking around home this weekend. My granddad had another stroke, and they don't expect him to last more than a few days."

That was news to me. I didn't even know I had a great-granddad. Mom probably told me, but I get all those people confused. There are a bunch of great-aunts and great-uncles, and then there's another bunch on my dad's side of the family that I've never even met.

Cindy said, "Oh, that's a shame. Were you close to him?"

"No, not really," Mom said. "I haven't seen him for years, but of course I'll have to go to the funeral. I'm dreading that."

Cindy used her fakest-sounding voice and said, "Yes, family funerals can be so sad."

"Well, it's not that so much," Mom said. "I mean, he's ninety-three years old and he's been bedridden for years and doesn't recognize anyone except his canary. What bothers me is . . ." She lowered her voice. "Zelda."

"Why?" Cindy whispered back. "Are you afraid she'll be emotionally damaged by her first experience with death?"

"No," Mom said, "I'm afraid she'll do something terrible and humiliate me in front of all those aunts and uncles.

She's never been to a funeral before. We don't even go to church. Zelda is a sweet kid, and I love her a bunch, and she really does try to be good. But somehow she just seems to cause calamities wherever she goes. I can just see her knocking over the casket, or bursting out laughing at a solemn moment, or something like that."

"I would not," I called out in my maddest voice.

They were dead silent.

"I thought you were cleaning your room." Mom said. There was low thunder in her voice.

I stomped up the hall and went into my room. But I didn't clean it.

I sat on my bed and thought. I was mad at Cindy on general principles and mad at Mom for not trusting me. But I was also a little bit scared. Mom was right. I did get into a lot of trouble, most of it when I was trying my hardest not to. What was I going to be like at a funeral, for heaven's sake?

I decided I'd better do something about this situation right now.

I got up and put on my best dress.

ᕲ

I was okay till I got to the funeral home. It was three blocks from my house, and all the way over there I told myself that this was going to be easy. Just a trial run, a dress rehearsal for the funeral Mom was going to have to take me to pretty soon. I figured if I was going to do something awful, I'd better do it at some funeral where nobody knew me.

How bad could it be? All I had to do was go in, sit down, be quiet, and leave when everybody else did. So I wasn't too scared . . . till I got to the Pearly Gates Memorial Home. *Then* I was.

It was a huge mansion. A palace. Like in the movies. It had marble columns out in front, and bushes trimmed into perfect circles, and great big doors.

I stood outside, trying to decide whether I should really be doing this.

Then a couple walked past me and the big door opened, and a man in a dark gray suit welcomed them. It looked pretty in there, from what I could see through the door. I started getting more curious than scared.

Some more people came past, a married couple and two older kids. I fell into step just behind them and went in.

The man in the dark gray suit drifted up to us from out of the shadows. He had the slicked-downest hair I'd ever seen, and a voice so soft and low you had to lean toward him to hear anything. I got a little closer. He didn't move his lips when he talked, and I wanted to see how he did that.

"You're with the Wickersham party?" he murmured, and the people I was following said yes.

"Parlor A," he said. At least the sound came from him, but you couldn't have proved it by his lips.

The rest of the family went on into another room, but I held back to look around. I was in a big square room with soft green carpet and old-fashioned wallpaper and a marble fireplace. The lights were low and soft, and there was churchy music coming from some-where. It was a terrific room.

I went over and tried to see up the chimney of the fireplace but my neck wouldn't bend enough. I got down on my hands and knees and stuck my head clear in. Sure enough, I could see a teeny little bit of blue sky up at the top.

Gray Suit's feet appeared beside me. "You'd better go on in with your family, now," he said. I've never been scolded in such a soft, beautiful voice before. I took my head out of the fire-place to watch his lips not move while he said, "The Wickersham party, I believe."

"Do they have a party at funerals?" I asked, standing up and acting dig-nified.

He gave me a look like I'd stepped on his foot. I didn't see why. It seemed like a perfectly reasonable question to me.

He stared me down.

"Parlor A," he said.

"Parlor A." I cleared my throat and marched through the door my "family" had gone through.

The room was like a little theater, with rows of folding chairs and soft lights. But instead of a stage at the front, there was a casket. The real thing. A genuine dead person up there.

I sat down in the last row, by myself. I figured I couldn't get into any trouble *there*, and as soon as it was over I'd just leave. I was beginning to wish I'd taken time to find the bathroom before I'd come in, but I didn't want to get up and go back out through the fireplace room and have Gray Suit frown at me again.

So I sat very lady-like with my ankles crossed and my hands holding each other in my lap. I didn't swing my feet or kick the chair in front of me or anything. I looked around. There were big baskets of flowers along the sides of the room. They smelled like Cindy. And up front—the casket.

It was shiny white with sparkly gold designs on it. Half of the lid was closed, and the other half was open. Kind of like a sleeping bag. The inside of the open part of the lid was all fluffy white satin. It looked very comfortable. But I couldn't see the dead person at all, and it was just as well.

About half of the folding chairs were full, and people were turning around to talk and whisper back and forth. I figured the main part of the funeral hadn't started yet.

I stretched my ears and listened to them, to get an idea of what it was okay to talk about at a funeral.

"Well, Frank, I said to him, your brother is a night manager at Hardees. If he can afford . . ."

"Look over there. Isn't that Joe's oldest girl? Is that her husband? I heard he was a strange one. He's wearing an earring. One earring. Well, that side of the family, what can you expect?"

"Is that Evelyn over there to the right? That can't be Evelyn. That woman must weigh three hundred pounds. Yes, sir, that *is* Evelyn. Well, she's certainly let herself go."

"Which side of the family are you with?"

The last voice was close to my right ear. In fact, it was aimed at me. A middle-aged couple had come into my row from the other side, and sat one chair away from me. The woman was looking down at me, smiling and waiting for an answer.

"Um," I said. *Think fast,* I told myself. But I couldn't.

The woman's husband peered around her, looking me up and down. He said, "She's got to be one of Joe's clan. That funny-colored hair, that comes from Joe's side."

"I am not from Joe's side," I said, as coldly as I could. There was nothing wrong with the color of my hair. My hair was the color of cookie dough at sunset, and it was a lovely color.

The man and woman stared at each other. She said, slowly, "Well, if you're not from our side, and you're not from Joe's side, you must be from . . ."

I waited, breathless.

The man said, "She must be from Alice's side." He said it with such awe that I decided I would be from Alice's side. It sounded better than Joe's or theirs.

"Yes. I am from Alice's side."

The woman twisted around in her chair to face me. "You're from Alice's side?" Her voice attracted attention from three rows ahead of us, and heads turned.

"Yes," I said, trying to talk softly and liplessly like the Gray Suit.

The lady beside me said, "You can't be Alice's . . ."

"I am Alice's daughter," I said with great dignity.

The man snorted. "Alice is seventy-eight years old. And she's never been married."

I held my head up proudly. "She was secretly married and never told any of her relatives. Because she didn't like them," I added spitefully. These people were getting on my nerves.

The man, who was nobody's fool, said, "If you're really Alice's daughter, where is Alice? What are you doing here alone, all the way from Michigan?"

I held my head even higher. "Alice, my mother, was busy this weekend. She's having dinner with the president, so she sent me instead. She thought one of us should be here for the funeral."

I could see from their faces that they didn't believe that part about the president, so I added, "Not the president of the country, the president of—um—the school board."

They looked at each other again, and the woman said, "She does have

Alice's eyes, don't you think? That funny sort of blue color?"

First my hair, then my eyes. I could see why Alice didn't have anything to do with these people. She was too good for them, and so was I.

"She let you come all this way by yourself, a little child like you?" the woman said.

"Alice trusts me. Mother, I mean. I'm very advanced for my age."

I was getting in deeper and deeper. Just then, the background music stopped, and a man who looked like a minister walked to the front of the room.

Hooray, I thought. *I can't get into any trouble just listening to a sermon.*

☾

The man and lady beside me whispered that they were my cousins Margaret and Arthur Wickersham. He kept giving me slant-eyed looks, like I wasn't fooling him, but Cousin Margaret seemed thrilled with the idea that I was Alice's surprise daughter. I just wanted them to get off the subject.

The minister went "Ahem," and everybody quit looking around at their relatives and shut up for the sermon. First they sang a hymn about somebody named Amazing Grace. I didn't sing since I didn't know the song. I just listened to the words and tried to figure out who Grace was, and why she was so amazing. The song never did say why.

I sang quietly to myself, "Amazing Zelda, how sweet thou art."

The minister gave a little talk about heaven. I was right. I didn't get into one bit of trouble all through his whole speech. Every once in a while I'd catch Cousin Margaret looking at me. I'd give her my sweetest smile, and she'd look away.

After the sermon I thought it would be all over. I hoped so, because I was pretty serious about wanting to find the bathroom by that time. But no. There was more on the program.

Some man—I think he was the Joe whose side of the family I didn't belong to—came up to the front and gave a speech about the dead person. He kept saying how wonderful she was.

"She was a tight-fisted old battle-ax," Cousin Margaret whispered to me. "She was so cheap she'd breathe through her nose to save wear and tear on her false teeth."

I nodded and looked straight ahead. I was being incredibly good.

Somebody else got up and gave another little speech about how wonderful Mrs. Wickersham was. That was the name of the departed, as they kept calling her. I hoped this one was going to be the last speech. I figured there was probably a bathroom somewhere down the hall.

Finally the minister started to wrap

things up, but Cousin Margaret raised her hand, just like a kid in school.

"Yes?" the minister said.

She stood up. "We have a very special young guest with us today. This little lady here beside me is Alice Wickersham's daughter." She looked down at me.

"Zelda," I said, with a feeling of doom.

"Alice's daughter, Zelda, who has come all the way from Michigan, all by herself, just to attend her aunt's funeral. I think we should have her say a few words."

Oh no. Everyone turned around and stretched their necks to stare at me. I shook my head, but Cousin Margaret gave me a little shove and said, "Go on, dear, just say a few words."

I dragged my feet all the way up to the front, looked away from the casket of the departed, and stared at the audience. I can't even stand up in class to give a book report without practically throwing up with nervousness. Here I was with all these relatives staring at me, waiting to see what kind of fool Alice's daughter was.

So for Alice's sake, for the honor of our whole side of the family, I made up a speech.

"I didn't ever meet the departed, since I live in Michigan with Alice and her secret husband. But I know the departed took very good care of her teeth. Thank you."

I sat down, smiling at how well I did. *Now,* I thought, *it's all over and I can go find the bathroom.*

The minister raised us up for a final hymn. Then he said, "The interment will be at the Pleasant Grove Cemetery. If you'll just file out through the front here, and out this side door, we'll form the procession. And I think this young lady should lead the way."

Oh no.

Smiling like he was doing me an

honor, he grabbed me by the elbow and led me past the casket. I didn't look in.

Everyone fell into line behind me, and we paraded slowly out the side door into the sunshine. The minister turned me over to Gray Suit and said, "This young lady came all the way from Michigan, all by herself, for her aunt's service. I think she should ride in the lead car, don't you?"

"Oh, no, that's okay," I said modestly, trying to get out of his grasp. But they were too much for me. Before I knew what was happening, I was sitting in the great big back seat of the longest, blackest car in the world.

"Where are we going?" I asked Gray Suit, who slid in behind the wheel.

"Why, to Pleasant Grove Cemetery, for the graveside service," he said.

"Do they have a bathroom there?" I asked. But he didn't hear me, and I was afraid to say it again any louder.

ᖇ

I turned to look out the back window of the car. Behind us was the longest parade I'd ever seen, six more long black cars all with their headlights on, even though it was bright daylight. And they all had little black flags flying from their aerials. Behind them came a whole line of ordinary cars, with lights and flags too, so I knew they were with us.

We started off down the street, with a police car in front of us flashing his light. I sat back and tried to enjoy feeling important, but by then I really, really had to go.

"How far is it?" I asked Gray Suit.

"About twenty miles," he said. "It's out in the country."

Twenty miles. I'd never make it.

"Do they have rest rooms out there?"

He looked up at the rear view mirror. I could see his eyes looking at me. He didn't answer, but his look got darker and darker.

Finally I couldn't stand it any

longer. "We better find a gas station," I said.

"That's impossible. This is a funeral procession. We can't stop in the middle of a funeral procession."

"Well, I think we better," I said as calmly as I could.

I never saw anyone who could give that dirty a look through a rear view mirror. Without moving one bit of his face he said, "Why didn't you take care of that before we left."

"I didn't have a chance! I didn't want to come on this ride in the first place. You guys practically kidnapped me. I never wanted to give speeches or go to cemeteries. All I wanted to do was see what funerals are like. My mom is going to kill me when she finds out about this."

"What do you mean?" he asked like the voice of doom.

I shut up.

"You are a Wickersham relative, aren't you?" He sounded just like my school principal when you get caught in the hallway after the bell rings. Except the principal moves his lips when he talks. It's a lot more scary when nothing moves, and when it's coming at you through a mirror.

I cleared my throat. "I'm sort of an adopted member of the family. You might say."

"Adopted when?" Deep suspicion growled in his voice. He almost missed a turn, even though the police car was in front, leading us.

I cleared my throat again. "Well, I haven't been in the family too long." He stared at me harder, so I said, "Just since this morning."

"You *crashed* a *funeral?*" he said, and this time his lips actually moved.

"I was just practicing," I explained. "My mom was worrying about how I'd behave when my great-granddad dies, so I started worrying, too. I just thought I'd drop in and watch one of your funerals. So I'd know how to act, so my mom wouldn't get mad at me."

It sounded perfectly logical to me. But not to him, I could tell from the color of his face.

"You *CRASHED* a *FUNERAL?*"

"Well I didn't mean to!" I yelled. "And you didn't give me time to go to the bathroom before it started, and I didn't get a chance to after the sermons because people kept standing up and talking about the departed. And then that minister had me by the arm, and then you shoved me into this car, and now you're telling me it's twenty miles to the cemetery. Well, all I can say is we're going to be in really bad trouble if you don't find me a gas station *quick.*"

The car made a sudden swerve to the left, across the highway and into a Quick Pix station. I jumped out and ran.

When I came out of the restroom, everyone in the station was staring out the front window. I went to look, too.

There was my parade, stretching across the station, across the whole highway, all the way out of sight—six long black limousines, and all those other cars, headlights blazing, black flags flying. The police car had stopped and was holding up traffic in both directions. I could see a policeman waving cars to stop, with one hand, while he leaned over to talk to Gray Suit, probably trying to find out what the holdup was.

"What the devil is going on?" the station cashier said.

"Excuse me," I said politely, trying to squeeze past so I could get out the door. "That's my ride waiting for me."

I marched out proudly. Everyone in all those limousines was staring at me. Everyone in the station was staring at me. I waved at Cousin Margaret, in the car behind mine, but she didn't wave back. Cousin Arthur was yelling at her about something.

ᔕ

"And I don't want to see this child at Pearly Gates ever again," Gray Suit informed Mom. "Not ever, ever again, do you understand. I would prefer it if she crossed to the other side of the street when she passes."

He marched off and got into his long black car. I could see Mrs. Birdsall and several neighbors looking out their trailer doors. Perfect Paradise Trailer Park pays a lot of attention to what I do. I don't know why.

Mom pulled me in and shut the door. "When you left here, you said you were going visiting," she thundered. "Explain yourself, Zelda Marie."

I explained myself.

"I didn't really hurt anything, Mom. Mrs. Wickersham wouldn't have cared."

"Who is Mrs. Wickersham?" Mom yelled. "Or do I want to know?"

"Mrs. Wickersham was the departed. And believe me, it would have been a really dull funeral if I hadn't been there."

"Funerals are *supposed* to be dull, you pea-brain," she bellowed.

Then she simmered down, like she always does, and her face got to be a more normal color. "Okay, let's get this straight here, child of mine. You crashed this perfect stranger's funeral, just for fun?"

"No, not for fun. It *wasn't* fun. I did it for practice. You told Cindy you were afraid to take me to Great-Granddad's because I might do something terrible and embarrass you."

She didn't know how to answer that one.

"So I figured I should go to a different funeral first," I said. "That way, if I did anything awful, it wouldn't embarrass you."

She warmed up then, and hugged me into her stomach. "You're weird, Zelda Maria. You know that? You are thoughtful, in your own strange way, but definitely weird."

"I wasn't *bad*. They even asked me to make a speech at the funeral, and I did. A really good speech. You would have been proud of me. And it wasn't my fault I had to go to the bathroom in the middle of the funeral procession."

"I don't think I want to hear about that part," Mom said faintly.

Then she set me up straight and said, "While you were gone Aunt Mary called. Great-Granddad passed on, this morning, and the funeral is Tuesday at ten, in Omaha."

We looked at each other.

She cleared her throat and said, "I'd be glad to have you come with me, if you want to. It's up to you. I'm sure you learned a lot this morning, and I am not the least bit worried about your behavior."

I gave her the biggest hug I could and said, "I don't think I really want to go. I'd have to miss school. Maybe you'd better just leave me with Mrs. Birdsall while you go."

She thought about that a minute and said, "Now, Zelda, I'd be very glad to have you go with me. On the other hand, there are certain child psychologists who say it's not a good idea to take young children to funerals. They say it can have a damaging effect on them."

"We wouldn't want that, would we?" I said, shaking my head. She shook her head, too, and laughed a big, relieved laugh.

2. Cupid Hammersmith

All I wanted to do was make Mrs. Birdsall happy, so she wouldn't be crabbing at me all the time. She lives in the trailer next to ours, and she takes care of me after school.

I was sitting in her living room trying as hard as I could to be good because she was having sinus. When she has sinus she goes around pinching the top of her nose and making faces every time I make a sound.

So I was sitting there reading a book. My foot started swinging, because my legs are too short to touch the floor.

I can't help it. My legs swing by themselves, and if something is in the way,
then sometimes my toe will start kick-
ing it. Just teeny little kicks that no one
can hear.

And besides, when you're reading a
book, you can't tell what your foot is
doing. If your toe is bouncing very quietly off the television or the back of the
chair, you don't even know about it because your mind is in the book.

But Mrs. Birdsall grabbed my ankle
and said I was giving her a sinus head-
ache, and I had to sit like a lady. It was
awful. My legs got numb from hanging
over the edge of the chair. And it was
raining, so I couldn't go out.

I told Mom about it when she got
home from work. Her friend Cindy was
there, hanging around. You know
Cindy, the one with the big woolly false
eyelashes and enough perfume to gag a
horse.

Mom said, "You'll just have to try to
put up with Mrs. Birdsall, Zelda. She's

a lonely old lady, and she hasn't had a very happy life since her husband died."

"What that woman needs is a love life," Cindy said. "Believe me. The right man would do wonders for her."

I thought about that. I thought, *maybe* . . .

Then I thought, *nah.*

Then I thought, *maybe* . . .

Then I thought, *nah.*

Then I decided to give it a try. Anything that would make Mrs. Birdsall uncrabby would be worth whatever effort it took.

I told my best friend Kimberley about it while we ate lunch the next day. We always sit together at the second-to-the-last table in the school cafeteria, with Brinda Burgess across from us. Brinda is very big for her age.

It was Friday, so lunch was tuna casserole and a teeny little square of wiggly orange jello, one triangle of bread and butter, and a carton of chocolate milk. It didn't take long to polish that off. Then we got down to serious talking.

"Where can I find a boyfriend for a really old lady?" I asked Kimberley. "Mrs. Birdsall is always crabbing at me, and Mom and Cindy think it's because she needs a boyfriend." We giggled a while at the idea of anybody wanting a tall, skinny old lady with sinus headaches for a girlfriend.

"Help me think of some ideas," I insisted.

Kimberley is the only person I know who can finish off the milk in the bottom of the carton without making a sound with her straw. It's impossible. I've tried it, and I know it's impossible, but Kimberley does it. She did it just then. I watched and watched, but I couldn't see how.

Brinda was so messy she couldn't even open the milk carton without spilling half of it on her tray.

Kimberley said, "What you need is an escort service. You know, one of those places where you call up and order a date, and they send somebody over. Rich ladies in Florida use them all the time. I saw it on television."

"My uncle is an escort driver," Brinda said.

Usually I try not to look at Brinda while we're eating because she's so messy, but she got my attention this time.

"Your uncle is an escort? Really? You mean I could call him up and get him to come over and take Mrs. Birdsall out on a date?"

She looked a little blank. "I guess so. If that's what an escort is. I know he goes out on escort trips all the time."

"Is he old?" Kimberley asked.

Brinda shrugged. "I guess so. He's my uncle."

"Do you know his phone number?" I whipped out my Snoopy spiral notebook.

"No, but his name is Burt Burgess. I think he lives somewhere around Riverside."

It was still raining that afternoon, but this time I didn't mind being shut in with Mrs. Birdsall. I kept looking at her and grinning, thinking about the great surprise I had for her. She'd look back at me, suspiciously, trying to figure out what I was grinning about. But she didn't ask, and I didn't say.

She was working at the kitchen table over some spread-out newspapers. She had glue and pine cones and little bits of green and red felt and little circles of wood. I sat quietly at the table, not touching anything. I asked what she was doing.

"I'm making turkey table favors for the Thanksgiving dinner at the church. The glue is sticky, dear, so don't touch anything."

Of course the glue was sticky. What good would it be if it weren't? But I kept the smile on my face. I could hardly wait for her to get her new boyfriend.

"Mrs. Birdsall . . ."

"Yes, dear. Don't touch those, they're still drying."

"Do you like to go out on dates?"

She jumped and looked at me like I'd said something shocking. "I haven't gone out on a date in forty years. Not since before I was married. Where do you get such strange ideas?"

"But wouldn't you like to, if you could?"

She laughed the kind of laugh old people do when they don't know the answer to your question.

"Wouldn't you?" I pressed on.

"Oh, possibly. If the gentleman were suitable."

I made a mental note to tell the escort man to wear a suit.

"Where would you like to go, if you did go out on a date?" I was being very cagey. She thought we were just having a conversation. She didn't know I was pumping her for vital information.

She stopped spreading glue on a pine cone and threw her head back to think. She can always think better when her sinus is back like that.

"There used to be a place my husband and I went when we were courting. The Starlight Ballroom. It was down by the river, at the end of Broad Boulevard. I think it's still there, although I don't suppose it's open anymore. Not since Glenn died."

"Was that your husband?"

She shot me a what-a-stupid-question look. "I was referring to Glenn Miller, the famous band leader. He used to play at the Starlight Ballroom, and my husband Edmund and I would dance till dawn."

I found it hard to believe she would ever do something like that. But it made me feel good. I was going to give her back the good old days.

Zelda, you're terrific, I told myself. And by this time tomorrow night, Mrs. Birdsall would be saying it, too.

☉

I had to wait till "Dallas" came on television to make my phone call. When "Dallas" was on, Mom never heard anything going on in the real world.

I took the phone around the corner into the bathroom along with my Snoopy notebook and the telephone book. Making myself comfortable on the floor under the sink, I went into the match-making business.

I dialed, and a man answered.

"Is this Burt Burgess, the escort?"

He paused a minute, and said, "Yes. Who wants to know?"

"My name is Zelda Hammersmith. I'm a friend of Brinda's, and I want to hire an escort for Mrs. Birdsall. She's the lady who takes care of me after school."

He paused again, thinking. "Why isn't this Mrs. Birdsall calling me herself, and why are you calling *me* instead of the company. I just work for the company, you know."

Patiently I explained. "She doesn't know about this. It's supposed to be a surprise. I want you to come tomorrow night and take her to the Starlight Ballroom. She lives in Perfect Paradise Trailer Park."

"Oh," he said, "she lives in a trailer. Oh, well, now I get you."

I scowled, trying to figure out what he meant by that.

"You want me with the full rig, then," he said.

I guessed he meant wearing a suit and tie, so I said yes.

"Now let me get this straight. You want me to haul a Mrs. Birdsall from the trailer park to the Starlight Ballroom. Tomorrow night."

"Yes, please. Come about six o'clock."

"That's kind of an odd time. Oh well, Jake and me do a lot of moonlighting. That's no problem."

"Who's Jake?" I asked, suspiciously.

"He's my partner. I can't do it alone, you know. I'm just the escort driver."

I was getting in over my head here. "Fine," I said. "You and Jake, six o'clock, Lot Twelve, Mrs. Birdsall. And be sure to wear your full rig."

I hung up the phone. *Good,* I thought, *she'll be getting two instead of just one. Then she can choose whichever one she likes better.*

☾

The next afternoon was sunny at last, after all that rain, so I had to go outside and run off my energy. It was Saturday, and tonight was going to be Mrs. Birdsall's big night, so I was full of bounce. I ran the five blocks to the park, thinking I'd climb around on the monkey bars a while, but they were all full of little kids.

I walked along looking for something to do. I wished Kimberley was with me. She had ballet class on Saturday afternoons, which was a big pain in the neck for me. What good is a best friend who can never do anything on Saturday afternoons?

So I was walking along thinking about Mrs. Birdsall's big date tonight, and I started worrying. What if she didn't like either Burt or Jake? What if she thought it wasn't romantic enough, just calling up and ordering an escort over the phone?

I decided I should keep my eyes open and see if I could find any more possibilities for her. Almost as soon as I decided that, I spotted one.

He was old like Mrs. Birdsall, and he had a nice round rosy face, especially his nose. His clothes were kind of dirty and torn, but at least he was wearing a suit, and she did say the man had to be suitable. She didn't say clean-suitable.

He was sitting hunched over, staring at his feet. I went over to him and said hi.

He gave me a dirty look and said, "You shouldn't talk to strange men in the park, little girl."

"Are you strange?"

"I certainly am. At least, that's what my family says. My daughters and their husbands. Stupid people, every one of them. Slaving their lives away for the great god Money. Charging everything they own on credit cards. Arguing about who's going to inherit what, when I die. So you know what? I got back at them. I spent it all. I haven't got two nickels to rub together. How do you like that?"

"Why would you want to rub two nickels together?"

"Ah," he said, looking at me more kindly. "Wisdom from the mouths of babes. Why indeed. Why rub two nickels together?"

This was getting a little beyond me, so I got down to business. "How would you like a nice old lady for a girlfriend?"

He laughed. "No thanks, kid. That apartment building where I live, it's nothing but man-crazy old widows. They think I've got money, see, but I don't. I fooled them, and I fooled my kids. I spent it all, and I'm not telling what I spent it on. And now I'm a bum sitting in the park all day. I used to be a stockbroker, you know that?"

I frowned. "You mean like a cowboy? Breaking horses and stock and stuff like that?"

He laughed like I'd told him a good one. "Bulls and bears, I was breaking. Bull markets and bear markets, I survived them all, and now I'm a bum in the park and no one's going to get me off this bench. This is where I belong."

I sat down beside him. "You had bulls and bears?" He was beginning to sound too good for Mrs. Birdsall. Maybe I'd keep him for my own friend.

"The stock market," he explained. "It's bullish when prices are going up, and it's bearish when prices are going down."

Oh. That wasn't so interesting. I decided Mrs. Birdsall could have him after all. If I could get him there.

"Will you come home with me and meet Mrs. Birdsall?" I said.

"No thanks. I got enough old ladies chasing after me as it is."

I thought. "Okay," I said. "Then I'll just have to keep on talking to strange men in the park till I find one who will."

"No, you don't. That's dangerous. This Mrs. Birdsall shouldn't be letting you run around loose like this. If she's your sitter, she should be taking better care of you. Come on, I'll walk you home and give her a piece of my mind."

I didn't bother to tell him she didn't take care of me on Saturdays. I was just glad to get him going with me. This way Mrs. Birdsall could take her choice— Burt or Jake or . . .

"What's your name?" I asked him as we started out of the park.

"Puddin' Tame. Ask me again and I'll tell you the same."

That was silly. "What is your name really?" I insisted.

"Puddin' Tame. Ask me again and I'll tell you the same."

I could see he intended to keep that up, so I shrugged and gave in. If he wanted to be silly, it was all right with me. I just hoped Mrs. Birdsall would appreciate his sense of humor.

☉

We'd gone about a block toward home when an arm shot out in front of us and stopped us. The arm was wearing a black robe, and the hand was holding a booklet with a picture of an angel on it.

"Have you been saved?" a voice asked.

The arm and hand and voice belonged to a very skinny man with long hair down to his shoulders. He needed a shampoo. He wore a black robe that was open in front, so I could see jeans and a sweatshirt under it. It was a Minnie Mouse sweatshirt. I thought if he was trying to look like a preacher, he should have at least covered up Minnie Mouse.

Then I noticed his feet. They were bare. And they were the dirtiest feet I'd ever seen. Sometimes when I have to stay overnight with Mrs. Birdsall, she checks my feet before I get into bed, so I won't put dirty feet on her clean sheets. She'd have a wonderful time time cleaning this guy up.

"Have you been saved? Have you been born again?" he asked. He was talking to Puddin' Tame, or whatever my bum's name was, but Tame wasn't answering, so I did.

"I was born once. Isn't that enough?"

"Innocent child," the hairy man said. "Innocent child, you carry all the sins of mankind in your soul. You must be born again."

"No thanks," I said. "I don't think I want to go through that again."

"But you carry the sins of mankind in your soul."

"No, I don't. Well, there was that one time when I tried to get my neighbors arrested, but I really did think they were selling black-market babies. So that wasn't really a sin. And I didn't mean to crash Mrs. Wickersham's funeral. And I can't help it if my feet kick the backs of other people's chairs. I don't even know my feet are doing it. And that time . . ."

He was looking down at me now. "Innocent lamb, you are starting early on the road to perdition. What is your earthly name, child?"

My earthly name? "Zelda Hammersmith," I told him. That's about as earthly as you can get. "What's yours?"

"I am Brother Salvation." He tried to hand me another booklet.

"That's not your earthly name, right?"

"It's my heavenly name. My earthly name was Calvin Buttsky."

"Well, I can see why you changed it. Listen, would you like to meet a really nice lady? I don't think she's been born more than once, and that was a long time ago. Maybe she'd like to have her soul saved."

What the heck, I thought. *Might as well give her lots to choose from.*

"I will save souls wherever I find them," Brother Salvation said, and he fell into step beside Tame and me.

"What about you, sir?" Brother Salvation said. "Have you been born again in the grace of the Lord?"

Tame knocked Brother's hand off his arm. "Don't waste your energy trying to save my soul. I was on Wall Street for forty years. I'm beyond hope. I don't plan to die, anyway. It would give my family too much satisfaction. I'm going to be a bum on a park bench forever, just to get even with them."

"Vengeance is mine, sayeth the Lord," Brother quoted.

"Vengeance is mine, too, buddy,"

Tame snapped. "They all think they're going to inherit a bundle. Let me tell you, they are going to get zip! Zip. Nothing. Zero. I spent it all." He cackled.

A block from home I spotted another possibility. He was sitting on one of the lawn chairs outside the Green Pastures Retirement Home. He looked a lot older than the other boyfriends, but I thought that might be good. I didn't know how old Mrs. Birdsall was, but her neck was awful wrinkly, and so was this man's. I left Tame and Brother Salvation arguing on the sidewalk and went across the grass to the old man.

"Hi," I said.

He looked up at me. "Why, Ethel, it's you."

"No, it isn't. It's Zelda Hammersmith. I live over at Perfect Paradise, and I was wondering . . ."

"Sorry," he said. "Everybody looks like Ethel these days. I was in love with Ethel, back in aught-twenty. She'd never have anything to do with me, though. Said she didn't like the way I parted my hair. Couldn't say that now, could she?" He cackled and pointed to his bald head.

"Would you like to meet a nice lady? She needs a boyfriend so she won't be crabby when she takes care of me. I've got these two," I lowered my voice and nodded toward Tame and Brother, "but they might be too young for her."

He started working at getting himself out of his chair. "Sure thing, toots. I haven't had a new lady friend since way back in aught fifty or aught sixty. These old birds in the retirement home, they're all over the hill, you know? I need a lady with a little pep left in her. Know what I mean?"

I wasn't sure I did. I wasn't sure I wanted to. But he was cute anyway, so I brought him along.

Orville, he said his name was. I introduced him to the others.

"Don't leave your relatives anything," Tame advised him. "They'll get greedy and start fighting among themselves. Not worth it. Take my advice. Spend it all on yourself. That'll teach 'em."

Brother Salvation said, "Have you been born again, my friend? If not, we'd better hurry. You don't look like you've got much time, if your soul hasn't already been saved."

Orville cackled in his face. "Better men than you have tried, you long-haired wimp. Tried and failed."

He poked his cane into Brother Salvation's Minnie Mouse, and almost knocked him over.

The afternoon was getting late and cool and dim. Almost six o'clock, I figured. Better get these guys to Mrs. Birdsall so she could look them over before Burt the Escort got there.

I skipped a little ahead of my three finds. This was going to be fun. I could hardly wait to see Mrs. Birdsall's face.

☾

We had to walk very slowly because Orville could only take short steps, so it was almost dark by the time we turned in at Perfect Paradise. Something was going on at Mrs. Birdsall's.

An old brown Ford with a flashing light on top had just stopped in front of Mrs. Birdsall's trailer. Following the Ford was a huge truck, at least the front end of a huge truck, just the cab part. As I ran forward, the man in the Ford got out and walked up to the front door.

"Are you Mrs. Birdsall?" he asked.

If this was Burt the Escort, I was disappointed in him. He was wearing overalls, not a suit. And he looked way too young for her. I was glad I'd brought Tame and Brother Salvation and Orville.

Mrs. Birdsall was standing out in front of her trailer.

"Yes," she said slowly, looking around. She spotted me and my three men. Then she spotted the truck cab.

Then she spotted the man getting

out of the cab and pacing around the side of her trailer, thumping its metal skirts.

"What's the meaning of this?" she asked down her long nose and through her sinus.

"We're the movers," Burt told her. "Jake," he called, "the gas connection is over on this side. You get that and I'll disconnect the electricity."

"Now just one minute here, young man," Mrs. Birdsall said loudly. "You keep your hands off my connections. There's been some mistake."

I figured I'd better get in and straighten it out. "Burt," I said. "I'm the one that called you. You were supposed to be wearing a suit, you and Jake. You can't go dancing in overalls."

"What dancing?" He stared down at me like I'd said something very odd. "Look. You called and ordered a haul job and an escort driver. That's him, that's me."

Brother Salvation came up behind me and said to Mrs. Birdsall, "Ma'am, have you been born again in the light of the lamb?"

"What?" she yelled. I didn't know Mrs. Birdsall could yell.

Mom came running over, and she wanted to know what was going on. I wasn't so sure, myself.

"Burt," I said, "How come Jake brought that big truck?"

"To move the trailer, of course," Burt shouted down at me.

"But I didn't want you to move her trailer. Where did you get that idea?" I can yell, too, if I have to.

"You ordered an escort driver!"

"Yes! To take Mrs. Birdsall out dancing."

Tame came up then, and said, "Listen, lady, if you haven't made your will yet, take my advice. Spend it all yourself. Don't leave it to your relatives."

"Wait a minute," I said to Burt.

"What is an escort driver, anyhow? Isn't that somebody who takes ladies out on dates?"

"Zelda Marie," Mom screeched. "What on God's green earth have you done this time?"

Burt squatted down on my level so we could talk since there was so much yelling going back and forth over our heads.

Brother Salvation called to Mom. "God's green earth, that's right. But we live only a short while in this vale of tears. You must be born again so your soul can enter heaven."

Burt said, "I think we have a little problem here, kid. See, what I am is an escort driver. That's the guy who drives the car with the light on it." He waved toward the Ford with the flashing light. "I go in front of the rig, there, when Jake is hauling a wide load, like a trailer. That warns the other cars that a wide load is coming, so they can get out of the way. That's what an escort driver is, see?"

"Oh . . ." I said. "*That's* what an escort driver is. Oh, I get it now."

"Stop that," Mrs. Birdsall screamed at Jake, who was pulling the metal skirts off the bottom of the trailer.

Orville sidled up beside her. "Say there, I like your spirit. What's your name?"

Tame yelled, "Puddin' Tame. Ask me again and I'll tell you the same." He laughed like he was having fun.

Brother Salvation went over by Mom and tried to hand her a booklet. "It's right here in the scriptures, Sister. Ye shall drive the devil out of your soul, and ye shall . . ."

"Oh, shut up!" Mom hollered.

Burt stood up and yelled, "Jake, leave it. False alarm. This stupid kid thought we were a dating service."

Mrs. Birdsall turned on me. "A what? A dating service? Zelda Hammersmith, you will be the death of me yet."

Tame said, "Well, just be sure you spend it all before you go. Don't leave those blood-sucking relatives of yours one single nickel. They didn't earn it; they don't deserve it."

"But you must give your soul to the lamb." Brother Salvation came flapping over in his long robe, having given up on Mom.

"She ain't cashing in yet," Orville said stoutly. "Me and her are going to go out and boogie. Ain't that right, Ethel?"

"I'm not Ethel!"

"Neither am I," I chimed in. I wanted to get in on the yelling.

Just then another flashing-light-car pulled up. Two policemen who looked familiar got out and came over.

"What's the trouble here?"

"No trouble, officer," Burt said. "We were called out here to move this trailer, but . . ."

"Let me see your permit," the policeman said.

His partner looked down at me and said, "Uh-oh, Sarge. It's that kid again. That's the one who got us out here on the fake ambulance call and the fake child-selling call."

I eased around beside Mom.

Quite a few of the neighbors were out by that time, standing around listening and trying to look like they weren't listening.

Burt explained things to the policemen, and they muttered a while. Then they yelled, "Break it up now," at the circle of neighbors, and finally they drove off.

Burt and Jake put the trailer skirting back on and left. It looked to me like Burt was laughing, but I wasn't sure.

Mom looked down at me, and I looked down at my feet.

At the edge of the crowd I heard Brother Salvation say, "Ma'am, have you been born again?"

And someone answered, "Oh, yes, brother. I've been saved, I've been saved."

"Hallelujah," he said, and they disappeared together, Brother's robe flapping open and uncovering Minnie Mouse.

Orville was still in there pitching. "Come on, Ethel, get on your glad rags. You got a car? We can go down to the Starlight Ballroom and cut a rug."

Glad rags? Cut a rug? And they think I talk funny.

"Get away from me," Mrs. Birdsall yelped. "You're an old man. Get away."

"Besides," Tame said, "the Starlight Ballroom is a warehouse now. Progress. The world is falling apart. I'm going back to my bench in the park. You coming?" he said to Orville.

"Might as well," Orville muttered. "No live ones in this crowd. Listen, I think you may have something. I've been saving my money, but I believe I'll just take your advice and blow it while I'm still spry."

They walked off together, taking very slow steps.

"Maybe a Caribbean cruise," Orville was saying as they disappeared into the night. "There's lots of live ones on those cruises."

෧

Mom took me home and gave me a very stern talk about picking up strange men in parks and at street corners and nursing homes.

"And besides," she said, "you had no right to try to interfere in Mrs. Birdsall's private life."

I hung my head in shame.

"If she wanted a gentleman friend I'm sure she could find one on her own, without your help," Mom said in her mother-voice. But I could see one corner of her mouth trying to hold down a smile.

"I was only trying to help," I said. "You and Cindy said she was crabby because she needed a love life. I was just trying to find her a few love lifes. And Brinda told me her uncle was an escort. That wasn't my fault. That was Brinda's fault."

Mom snorted softly. "Well, Zelda Marie. I just want you to promise me one thing. Two things. Three things."

"What?" Three was quite a few.

"One, you will not talk to strangers in the park, in public places, in private places, anywhere at all until you are twenty-one years old."

I nodded.

"Two, you will treat Mrs. Birdsall with the respect due to someone of her age, and you will never interfere in her private life again."

That one was easier. I nodded.

"And three. If I should ever decide to begin dating, you are never never *never* to bring me any bums, religious fanatics, or octogenarians."

I didn't know what that last one was.

"Or truck drivers," Mom added, fast.

I nodded.

As we went into our trailer Mom put her arm around me and hugged me into her stomach.

"Also," she said, "No Hindu snake charmers, no drug pushers, no punk-rock singers, no . . ."

3. Zelda Loses Her Head Completely

This week something wonderful happened. Mrs. Green's mother fell down and broke her hip. Well, of course that wasn't the wonderful part; that was the sad part. The wonderful part was that Mrs. Green had to go and take care of her mother.

I couldn't believe it when the principal announced that we would have a substitute teacher while Mrs. Green was gone. In the first place, I couldn't believe my good luck. Mrs. Green is twenty feet tall, and she hates kids. She always seems to hate me more than anyone else in the class, for some reason.

In the second place, I couldn't believe anybody as old as Mrs. Green could even have a mother. A mother is something you have when you're little, to take care of you. What would an old person like Mrs. Green do with a mother?

Of course I know in my head that old people still have mothers and fathers. I *know* that. I just don't believe it. Like that business about everybody having to die sooner or later. I know it, but I don't really-truly-honestly believe that I will ever die.

But what I started to tell you about was the wonderful thing that happened last week. Of course I got into a little bit of trouble over it, but it was still wonderful.

Mrs. Harmon. That was the wonderful thing that happened. Mrs. Harmon, our substitute teacher.

Everything about her was good, but some things about her were the best. One was that she smiled. A lot. I mean genuine all-over-the-face smiling, where her lips went up and came apart and everything.

The one time Mrs. Green smiled, her lips stayed together and just went straight back and down a little bit at one corner. Kimberley's brother said he saw her smile one time, and that was what it looked like. Otherwise I wouldn't have known for sure.

But Mrs. Harmon smiled all over her face. Her cheeks would push up so high she could hardly see out over them. Her nose would wrinkle up and her ears would flatten back. It was terrific.

And the best part of her smiling was that she did it at me! A lot—not just once or twice before she got to know me. That's happened to me before with substitute teachers. Mrs. Harmon looked right at me like she understood me . . . and smiled anyway!

Another wonderful thing about her was that she looked a little bit like me. She was sort of rounded all over, and not very tall for an old person. And she had hair the same color as mine. Cookie-dough color.

I thought maybe I could grow up to be like her—if I could ever get over my habit of getting into trouble. I'd like to be as smiley as she was, but it's hard to smile when people are yelling at you. If you do smile, they get even madder and yell even louder.

That was another wonderful thing about her. She never once yelled at me. She had a very quiet voice, so everyone in the class had to be quiet and lean forward to hear her.

Every day I could hardly wait to get to school. It was so nice to just sit there looking at her, listening to her not yelling.

After a couple of days I started having this dream. I dreamed she hugged me.

I dreamed she gave us a special assignment, and I did mine better than anybody in the class. I did so perfectly and wonderfully that she walked right down the aisle to my desk and picked me up and hugged me.

Every time I had this dream I would give her a big long smile, and she'd smile back at me. Sometimes she gave me a funny look, as though she didn't know why we were grinning at each other. But I kept doing it anyway, and she kept doing it, and it was the best week I ever had in school.

All week I kept looking for ways to do things for her. When she wanted somebody to pass back our test papers, I jumped up and grabbed them and passed them out so fast that nobody got their own papers.

When she asked if someone would help move the big table at the back of the room, I got there first. I was smiling like crazy, even though I had to knock Gerald into the globe to get there.

Every time I helped her with something, she would say, "Thank you, Zelda. That was very nice." Then I'd turn red and start dreaming about that hug some more.

And on Friday she did a wonderful thing. She gave us a special assignment!

"Now, class," she said in her soft voice, "I want you to do something for me."

I leaned forward and held my breath. Whatever it was, I was going to do it for her. Move tables, pass out papers, fall down dead in the ditch so she could walk over me—anything.

"Next Monday I want each of you to stand up and give me a little book report."

A book report. I could do that. I could give a whole *library* report if she wanted me to.

"Now I don't want you to write it out and just read it from a paper. I want you to pick a book or story that you especially like. I want you to tell me what the story is about, and why you liked it so much. You can think about it over the

weekend and plan what you're going to
say. Don't write it down; don't memo-
rize it. Just plan what you're going to
say. I want these book reports to be
short and informal, and . . . yes, Zelda?"

I was madly waving my arm.

"Will there be a prize for the best
one?"

Mrs. Green would have glared at me
and said, "This is a classroom, not a
county fair. We don't give prizes, we give
grades."

But Mrs. Harmon smiled like she
understood me. She said, "What kind of
prize did you have in mind?"

I turned very red. I couldn't say "A
hug," but that's what I was thinking.

Mrs. Harmon said in her soft voice,
"I will be very pleased with everyone who
does a good job."

That made me grin so hard I almost
pushed my cheeks off my face. She
understood me. I was going to get that
hug.

Even before the bell rang I was starting on a Plan. If my Plan worked out, my book report was going to be a hundred times better than anybody else's.

ɔ

On the bus after school Kimberley asked me what book I was going to do for my book report. I hadn't decided that part of the Plan yet, and I wasn't going to let her in on it anyway, so I said I didn't know.

"I think I'll do *A Very Young Dancer*. That's my favorite book."

Of course it would be. And if I wasn't careful, Kimberley might get ahead of me in the book report contest. She was so disgustingly neat she even gave neat book reports. She didn't say, "ah, um, uh," like most people. She just said words. It always came out sounding intelligent—but only because it didn't have all those other noises mixed in.

When she said she was going to do

a book about dancing, it made me want to be as opposite as I could possibly be. And the most opposite I could think of was *The Legend of Sleepy Hollow.*

I always loved that story anyway. That's where Ichabod Crane sees the ghost of the headless horseman galloping through the woods.

While Kimberley talked on and on about her dancing book, I was planning a mile a minute. My big Plan, the one I'd made back in school, was to dress up like a character from my book report. And now I had it!

I was going to give my book report dressed as the headless horseman.

ᔕ

It took Mom forever to get home from work that night. It always takes forever when I really need her. I sat at Mrs. Birdsall's and planned what I would say in my book report, and I watched out the window for Mom's car.

Then I had to wait another forever while she got un-tired from work. That meant she had to take off the jeans and sweatshirt she wore to her job and put on the jeans and sweatshirt she wore at home. Then she had to sit with her feet up while she drank a Mountain Dew and let her hands hang straight down. I guess stuffing sausages all day at the packing plant makes all the blood run up your arms or something.

Her at-home sweatshirt had a funny tongue on the front—sort of hanging out of the corner of a mouth. Under it, it said, "Physically pffft." I guess she *was* physically pffft because she never wanted to talk about anything tiring when she got home from work. At least not until she'd had her Mountain Dew and let her hands hang down a while.

Then when she started getting her energy back, she was too hungry to listen. I had to wait while she made sloppy

Joes. After we ate, I helped her clean up the kitchen. I thought that would be a good time to talk.

"I need your help, Mom. I have to make a costume for school Monday, for a book report."

"A costume? For a book report? That's getting fancy."

"I want to have the best book report in the class," I told her.

"Then why don't you just give the best book report? Why do you need to dress up in a costume? Is everybody dressing in costumes?"

"It's up to us. We only have to do it if we want to," I said. In a way that was true. I couldn't help it if nobody else thought of the idea.

Mom heaved a huge sigh that came all the way up from her toenails. "Okay. I wanted to be a mother. Nobody told me about all the school costumes it was going to involve, but now that I've got you, I guess I'd better do the job right.

What kind of costume? Something simple, right?"

"Right. All you have to do is make me look like my head's been cut off."

"Zelda Marie," she wailed.

Then "Dallas" came on, and we had to watch television without a word for a whole hour. I fell asleep on Mom, and I dreamed about Mrs. Harmon hugging me.

☉

By the next morning, Mom was muttering, "How do you get me into these things?" But she was beginning to get into the spirit.

She put one of her old suit jackets on me and fiddled around with it, pulling it up by the shoulders till the collar was above my head. Every time she did that, it jerked my arms straight out.

"Hmmm," she muttered.

She tried another jacket. It wasn't quite right either.

"I'll tell you what we need," she said finally. "We need a nice big man's jacket. One with roomy arm holes. Then all I have to do is make thick shoulder pads so it will stand up high enough. Why don't you check around the neighborhood and see if anybody has a man's jacket they'll give you."

I ran out, happy to have something to do with all my extra energy. First I tried Mrs. Birdsall because she used to have a husband. But she didn't have any of his jackets left.

I tried all the trailers on our side of the street. I didn't want to go over on the other side because Kimberley might see me and want to know what I was doing. I didn't want her in on this. If she found out I was dressing up for my book report, I knew for sure she'd show up in her butterfly costume from her dance recital.

Personally, I thought a headless horseman would outrank a butterfly. But I wasn't positive about Mrs. Harmon's taste in things like that. She might very well be the type who would go for a butterfly.

So I kept to my own side of the street. I didn't have any luck till I got to the very last trailer.

Mrs. Gunderson said she didn't have any suit jackets that she could give to me. She said her husband only had one good jacket, and he had too big a beer belly to fit into it anymore. But she wanted to keep it anyway so she could torment him for getting so fat.

She gave me his old bowling jacket, though. It didn't exactly look like anything the headless horseman would have worn, but it was a neat jacket. It was green and yellow, with a zipper up the front and a picture of a bowling ball knocking down three pins on the back. Over the bowling ball picture it said "Al's Body and Fender Shop."

I didn't understand what that had to do with bowling, or with Mr. Gunderson. Mrs. Gunderson explained that Al's Body and Fender Shop was the name of her husband's bowling team.

There's still a lot about older people that I don't understand.

"It's a great jacket," I said as I rolled it up in a ball. "Is it okay with your husband if you give it away?"

She laughed a nasty kind of laugh and said, "It'll serve him right for not taking me to bingo last Saturday night. If he wants to spend his whole life with those no-good friends of his at that no-good bowling alley, it's all right with me. It's fine with me. You never hear *me* complaining. *Oh* no, you never hear me say one word . . ."

I backed away while she was still talking, and I ran for home.

When I showed Mom the jacket, she said, "No, that's not the right kind. It has to be a suit jacket."

But I told her this was all I could get, so she shrugged her shoulders and gave in. I couldn't tell whether she was shrugging hopelessly or trying not to laugh out loud. Or both.

It took most of the afternoon, before she got it the way she wanted it. She made great big huge shoulder pads out of an ugly old throw pillow she didn't like. The pillow said "Greetings from Nashville," and since my dad ran away to Nashville to get famous, she hasn't liked greetings from there—not as much as she used to.

Next, Mom took a piece of cardboard and wrapped it into a kind of cone, stapled it together, and set it on my head so it looked like a skinny neck sticking out of the top of my head. She wrapped a white scarf around it to make it look even more like a neck.

Then came another tricky part. She dressed me in an old white blouse of hers that had a big flap of ruffles down the front. She hung it up around the fake neck and pinned it to the cardboard so that the ruffle flap was over my face.

Then, being very careful not to cut me, she took scissors and made slits between the ruffles so I could see and talk and breathe.

She put the jacket with the great big huge shoulder pads on me, zipped it up to my chin, and left the blouse ruffle hanging out, covering my face. Frowning, she looked at me, then got a black leather belt from her closet and put it around my waist to pull in the jacket and make it more like a headless horseman and less like a bowling jacket.

"Now," she said, "you're just about perfect. Wear your black tights and your cowboy boots, and you'll look just like a headless horseman. Too bad you don't have a horse."

I looked thoughtful.

"No, Zelda. Absolutely not. Whatever you are thinking, forget it. Absolutely no horses. Promise."

I tried to nod, but I was afraid of losing my neck.

Through the ruffles I said, "Now I

need a head. What can we use for a head?"

Mom starting dismantling me. "You're on your own for that part, toots. I've got Saturday chores to do."

My brain went into high gear. "Could I borrow your 'physically pffft' sweatshirt?"

"I suppose. Just don't ruin it."

It was a gray sweatshirt, pretty close to the color I figured a dead man's head would be. I took it to my room and went to work. First I stuffed it with my flannel nightgown and my Miss Piggy T-shirt. That made it about the right size and roundness.

I folded the sleeves inside, tucked up the bottom part so it wasn't too long, and tied the top and bottom off with string. That made it a round, head-sized ball with the tongue sticking out in just the right place, and the lettering all hidden.

Then I pinched up a big chunk of nose and tied it off with string, right above the tongue. With my marking pen I drew on a pair of very surprised-looking eyes and eyebrows. I figured that's the way a person would look right after his head got cut off.

For hair, I had the perfect thing—a long black straggly fright wig from my Halloween outfit. I pinned it on top of the sweatshirt with safety pins.

It was perfect.

Well, it was almost perfect. All it needed was lots of blood around the neck.

ↄ

I had so much stuff to carry on Monday morning that it took two big grocery bags to hold it all. Kimberley got mad at me because I wouldn't let her see what was in the bags, and she got up and went to the back of the bus and sat with Georgia Tripp. She can't stand Georgia, so I knew she did it to get back at me.

But that was okay. I was going to

give the world's greatest book report.

I was going to earn a hug from Mrs. Harmon.

I jammed the paper bags into my locker and shoved the door closed. We have very small lockers at Truman Elementary. Kimberley kept trying to stretch her neck to see what was in there, and I kept not letting her. I was happy to see she wasn't carrying anything that could have a butterfly costume in it.

Mrs. Harmon smiled at us all as we came into our room. I was pretty sure she smiled especially at me, like she knew what was coming.

My next worry was that she was going to make us wait till the end of the day for our book reports. I didn't think I could stand that. I'd been practicing what I was going to say, and I didn't want to forget it.

"My name is the Headless Horseman, and I'm a character from Zelda Hammersmith's favorite book, *The Leg-*

end of Sleepy Hollow." Then I'd go on and tell the story.

But I didn't have to wait all day. As soon as we got through with roll call and the Pledge of Allegiance and the announcements that come from the box up by the ceiling, we got right to it.

"All right, boys and girls. Your weekend assignment was to think of your favorite story and prepare to share it with the class. Who would like to go first?"

I waved my arm in the air.

She smiled. "Zelda?"

"I brought some things for my book report. May I be excused? They're in my locker."

Kimberley pricked up her ears.

"Yes, Zelda, you may be excused. But come right back. Gerald, we'll start with your report."

His would be awful. I grinned as I ran down the hall to my locker, got the bags, and took them to the girls' room.

It was a lot harder to get the neck

on with no one to help me. It kept slipping down over my eyes. Then I had a lot of trouble getting the blouse on right and pinning it to the neck. The slits didn't want to line up with my eyes and nose and mouth. They kept wanting to go off to the side.

The jacket helped hold everything together, though, especially after I put the belt on. But when I bent down to pull on my cowboy boots, the whole neck fell off, and I had to start over.

Finally I was all put together—except for the best part. The blood. I pulled out the ketchup bottle and shook it up. There hadn't been very much ketchup left in it, so I'd added some water and a whole bottle of some stuff called Worcestershire sauce.

I didn't even try to pronounce it.

The mixture looked pretty good. I shook up the bottle and poured some on the bottom part of the sweatshirt head. Then I tried to sprinkle just a little bit on my cardboard neck, but I couldn't

see what I was doing up there. I tried to
see in the mirror, but my hand kept
going the opposite way from where I was
aiming it.

I got a lot more blood on the neck
than I meant to.

Then from the bottom of the bag
came my last good thing. It was an old
horse's bridle. Last night I'd remembered the Sweeneys in the trailer park
who used to have horses. I asked them
if they had a whip I could carry so I
would look more like a horseman. They
said no, but they did have this old bridle
they'd kept for sentimental reasons
when their last horse died.

I figured it was the perfect touch.

So there I was, in all my glory. I
looked at myself in the mirror. I was perfect. Under one arm was my head with
the sticking-out tongue and the sur-
prised eyes and the wild black hair. In
my other hand was the old horse bridle.
My face was completely hidden behind
the ruffle, but I could see out pretty well.

At last. Time to make my grand entrance.

I felt my way out of the girls' room and bumped down the hall. The more I walked, the crookeder my eye slits got.

A classroom door opened in front of me and I bumped into someone. Whoever it was screamed.

I decided I'd better hurry up. Suddenly it seemed a very long way back to my classroom. Behind me I heard doors opening and voices sounding kind of shrill.

At last, the door to my own room. I was almost there when it opened and Mrs. Harmon came out.

She took one look at me and screamed and grabbed her throat. She sagged back against the door and kind of slid down till she was sitting on the floor, still grabbing her throat.

She wasn't smiling.

From behind me came the pounding feet of the principal. "Who's bleeding here? Who's bleeding here?" he yelled.

All the kids in my class ran to the door, and most of them screamed on top of all the other racket.

"What is this?" the principal kept hollering. He grabbed me by the arm and almost knocked my neck off.

"Hello," I said. "I am a character from Zelda Hammersmith's favorite book, *The Legend . . .*"

"Mrs. Harmon, are you all right?" The principal was trying to get her up off the floor, but he wasn't strong enough. And worst of all, she was crying.

From down the hall came the school nurse, galloping full tilt. "Who's bleeding? There's blood all the way down the hall to the rest room. I've got pressure bandages here."

Mrs. Harmon was crying. I dropped my head and my bridle and sat down beside her and gave her a hug.

೨

Well, finally it all got sorted out. The janitor came and mopped up the ketchup spots in the hall. The class went back to their seats, and Mrs. Harmon got herself up from the floor and stopped grabbing herself around the neck.

The principal started to give her a talking-to about keeping control of her classroom. But then he stopped. He looked at me for a while and patted Mrs. Harmon on the arm. He told her to hang in there, it was only one more week.

They made me take off my neck and jacket and blouse, but I did get to hold my head under my arm while I gave my report.

Mrs. Harmon said that she appreciated all the fine work and original thought that went into my presentation. And then she said, "Never, never again, Zelda!"

Kimberley was mad at me because nobody would settle down and listen to her dance book report after the excitement of mine. But she got over being mad. She always does.

When Mom got home from work that night she said, as she sat down with her Mountain Dew, "Well, how did the book report go?"

"It was a big success," I said carefully. "Mrs. Harmon told me she never saw a book report like it before."

Actually what she'd said was that she'd never been scared off her feet by a book report before.

And even though she didn't exactly give me a hug, I think she liked the one I gave her.

4. Zelda, the Red Hot Lemon Queen

I got into quite a bit of trouble last Saturday.

Saturday is supposed to be a kid's very best day of the week, right? I mean, all you have to do is maybe a little room cleaning, and if you live in a trailer, that's no big deal.

I can stand in the middle of my room and practically touch both sides of it. If I open the closet door at one end, go down to the other end, and throw my arms out and run, I can sweep up all the toys and junk and whoosh them right into the closet. Three minutes, tops, and I've got a clean room. A little dusting with the corner of the curtain and everything is perfect.

So usually Saturday is my favorite day. It seems like forever before I have to go back to school. The trouble with Sunday is that it's the day before I have to go back to school. I have to do my weekend homework, and there's a whole week of school days sticking up in front of my face.

But last Saturday was so crummy it might as well have been Tuesday.

For one thing, it was Veteran's Day. I've never understood Veteran's Day, and I don't want to. It's all about soldiers and wars, and the parade isn't nearly as good as the Fourth of July parade. It's full of jeeps and ugly, greeny-brown trucks, and a lot of men in soldier suits that don't fit them anymore.

It was a cold, cloudy, windy day. I couldn't get Kimberley to play outside with me, so I spent most of the morning on the floor watching dumb stuff on television while Mom vacuumed and cleaned the trailer.

The announcer said something about merchants predicting a record year in Christmas sales, and that got me thinking about my money problems. It's hard to get your mom a really nice Christmas present when all you have in your quarter bank is seven dollars, and all your money comes from her in the first place.

I started thinking about ways I could earn some money before Christmas. I was too little to baby-sit or get a regular job. My allowance never seems to make it from one week to the next, and I wasn't due to get any gift money from my grandmas till next spring.

"Up legs," Mom said. I lifted my legs, and she vacuumed under me.

"Mom," I said when she'd shut off the vacuum cleaner, "what other ways could I earn money besides my allowance?"

She put the vacuum cleaner back

in the hall closet and dragged the garbage can over to the refrigerator.

"What do you need money for? Don't I supply you with everything you could possibly want? Don't you already live the life of a fat cat on a cushion? Here, take a look at this."

She held out a little square plastic dish of leftovers. The leftover was a lump of something grayish and runny, and it had green fur around its edges.

We looked at each other.

I took my best shot. "Soup."

She sniffed. "No, I think . . . creamed something. What creamed food have we had in the last six months?"

"Maybe it's—I know," I yelled. "Pancake batter."

"Right on, Zelda. You win the Nasty Noseful Award of the week."

She dumped the gray blob into the garbage and went on with her search, in the back of the refrigerator shelves, for things too old to eat.

"How can I earn money?" I reminded her.

"Oh. Yes. Your cash-flow problem. You didn't tell me what you need it for."

"I can't tell you that. It's a surprise."

She looked at me suspiciously. "I just want to get you something nice for Christmas," I reassured her.

"Oh. Well, let's see. How could you earn money? When I was your age, kids had lemonade stands, but I suppose that's gone out of style by now."

"I guess so. I never heard of any of my friends doing that. How did it work?"

"Simple," Mom said, slamming the refrigerator door and pulling up the drawstrings on the garbage bag. "My sister and I used to do it in the summer. We'd get a couple of orange crates and boards, make a stand out of them, set it up in the front yard near the sidewalk, and put a sign on the front saying 'Lemonade, three cents.' "

"Three cents," I giggled. "I didn't know anything ever cost three cents."

"That was back in the dark ages, kid. We'd borrow a dollar from our mother to buy lemons and sugar, get a big bowl with ice, a bunch of paper cups, and we were in business. On a good hot afternoon we could make maybe a buck in clear profit. Dirty sheets."

We shifted the conversation to my bedroom while we stripped the sheets off my bed. This had been my week for the sheets with giraffes and rainbows. We kicked the giraffe sheets into the hall and put on the new ones. Kittens and ribbons. They were a present from my grandma who doesn't understand me very well. When I told her I'd like some Monster-Man sheets, she thought I was kidding.

While Mom went on to her own dirty sheets, I flopped across the kittens and ribbons for some serious planning.

A lemonade stand wasn't a perfect idea. For one thing, I didn't know how to make lemonade. For another thing, it was November, not the middle of a hot summer. For another, I was pretty sure there was no such thing as orange crates anymore. What could I make the stand out of?

But I loved a challenge.

I was pretty sure that somewhere in my fertile mind there were ways to make a lemonade stand in November, and ways to make a very large lot of money out of it. I might not be my grandma's idea of an average girl, but I was wonderful at coming up with plans.

And as I lay there on my kittens and ribbons, the Plan started putting itself together.

℧

After lunch, Mom left to go shopping and errand-running. Since she knew better than to leave me alone, I had my choice of going to Mrs. Birdsall's, going along on all the boring errands, or going to Kimberley's. I went to Kimberley's.

Her mother was out running errands, too. Her older brother was in charge, but he ignored us as hard as we ignored him. That worked out fine.

I told her about my plan for the lemonade stand and offered to cut her in on the profits if she'd help. She was standing in her bedroom in her ballet outfit, trying to make her arms into perfect circles over her head.

"What would I want to help you for?" she asked. "It's cold outside. I don't want to sit around in the cold all afternoon."

Plans were popping like popcorn in my mind by that time. "I don't want you to sit around," I said. "I want you to be the attraction. I want you to dance, to get people's attention so they'll stop and buy my lemonade. See?"

That got her. She started fishing

around in her closet for her butterfly costume.

"What are you going to use for a stand?" she asked from inside the closet.

I already had my eye on the perfect lemonade stand. Kimberley's dressing table. It was just the right size and shape, and it had a pretty white ruffly skirt all around it. That would give my lemonade stand *class*.

I looked under the skirt. It was mostly empty under there, just a couple of little drawers and skinny legs with those teeny wheels on their bottoms.

"Oh, no you don't," Kimberley said when she saw what I was doing. "You're not using my Dance Queen dressing table for a lemonade stand. I know you. You'll spill something on it."

"No, I won't. And if I do, I'll clean it up. You'll get it back in exactly the same shape as it's in now. Come on, Kimberley. You're supposed to be my best friend."

"You're supposed to be *my* best friend," she snapped, "and you never go to my dance recitals."

Well, that was true. I hated her dancing because I couldn't do it, and it made me feel like she was better than me. So I got even by not going to her dance recitals. But the more I looked at that dressing table the more I wanted it.

"Okay," I said. "You let me borrow your dressing table just for this afternoon, and I'll go to your next recital."

She gave me a steely look.

"Okay," I said. "Your next two recitals."

"Three."

I sighed. Three whole Saturday afternoons of watching her be a butterfly. "Okay, but you have to come out with me and be my attraction."

She was already getting into her butterfly outfit. It didn't have wings on the back. That would be babyish, she told me. But when she raised her arms up, there was a lot of thin, pink material that was supposed to look like butterfly wings.

We put on our warm boots and coats, although Kimberley had to hang her coat around her shoulders because of her wings. She liked to wear it around her shoulders anyhow. It made her feel like a big shot.

It took a lot of grunting and shoving and banging, but we finally got the dressing table rolled out through the hall, through the door, and down the steps to the sidewalk. Luckily her brother was practicing the French horn in his room with the door closed.

All the way down the trailer park sidewalk the dressing table rolled, its skirts flapping grandly in the wind. When we got out to the main sidewalk, we stopped while I thought.

"Let's go down in front of the National Guard Armory," I said. "That will put us right on the corner where all the cars go by."

We parked in the grass in front of the armory, and I left Kimberley to guard the dresser while I ran home.

I was in luck. Down in the bottom of the cupboard was the big cardboard carton of powdered lemonade mix from last summer. The next problem was finding something big enough to make it in. Mom didn't have any very big pans since she only cooked little stuff for the two of us.

Finally I found the perfect thing. It was in the back of the bathroom closet— a great big green plastic tub that Mom used sometimes to soak her feet when she had to work double shifts at the packing plant.

I washed it out in the bathtub so it would be nice and clean. Then I dumped the lemonade mix in and turned on the bathroom faucet. It worked fine. The stuff in the tub got more or less lemonade colored. When I tasted it, it tasted more like lemonade than like Mom's feet.

The problem came when I tried to pick it up. It was way way *way* too heavy for me. I had to scoop the lemonade into the two plastic pails Mom used for sponge-mopping the floor.

Grunting a lot, I started off down the sidewalk, a bucket in each hand and the green plastic tub upside down over my head. I could see out from under it if I tipped my head way back.

I decided I wasn't ever going to be a maid when I grew up. Water buckets could stretch your arms right out of your shoulders.

ᓚ

When I got to the stand, Kimberley was gone. But she came back right away with two things. Her school notebook and Derek. At least it looked like Derek in a rabbit outfit, walking along behind Kimberley.

Derek was younger than us. His mother thought he was the cutest thing since teddy bears, so she was always dressing him up. For Halloween she made him a whole pumpkin suit. Not just around his head, but around his whole body. He couldn't get through any doors with it when we went trick-or-treating, so he got twice as much candy as the rest of us. People felt sorry for him for having to stand outside when they invited us in.

This rabbit suit was left over from last Easter. He wore it in the Easter parade, and he kept fallling over the feet. The feet were very long and floppy. I could see how they'd be hard to steer around corners.

"What's he doing here?" I asked Kimberley. "And what's the notebook for?"

"The notebook is for making signs. And Derek wanted to know what I was doing in my butterfly costume. When I told him, he went home and got his rabbit suit. I don't want him doing rabbit things when I'm trying to dance."

"You can take turns," I said. I will probably be a very good executive when I grow up.

I set the green tub on the dressing table and poured the two buckets of lemonade in. Then I ran back home for a bucket of ice cubes and a stack of paper cups left over from Mom's card club.

By the time I got back, Kimberley had made a big sign by writing one letter on each page of paper from her notebook and pinning the pages on the dressing table skirt. L,E,M, and so on, all the way across. It looked great.

"How much are you going to charge?" she asked, her felt-tip pen poised over the paper.

I squinted and thought. "Thirty cents a glass." I figured that ten times what Mom charged would be about right, since it was a hundred years ago or so since she did this.

The sky was gray and low and cold looking. A nice hot sun would have helped a whole lot. I stamped around and hugged myself, waiting for business to start.

Business didn't start.

"Dance," I said to Kimberley. She dropped her coat and started doing twirly things up and down the sidewalk.

That should get some attention, I thought.

"I want to do something," Derek said from inside his rabbit head. His voice sounded funny in there.

"What do you want to do?"

"I don't know."

"What *can* you do?"

"I don't know."

Derek was a real pain. But if I was going to be a big-shot executive, I'd have to learn to handle these decisions. "Do somersaults."

He climbed up on the grass in front of the armory and tried to somersault, but his ears kept getting in the way. Finally, after a couple of tries, the ears weren't standing up all that much any-more, and he made better progress.

The trouble was, he'd learned to go over but not to keep rolling. He just flopped over and lay flat on his back, which meant I had to go pull him up after every somersault.

Probably big-shot lady executives don't have to do that.

Kimberley twirled past and said, without missing a twirl, "I don't want. Him doing that. While I'm dancing."

"He's making you look good by comparison," I yelled after her. Derek started crying. I was beginning to see why lady executives get paid so much. This was not an easy job.

But, nobody was paying me. No-body was even walking past on the side-walk. No cars were stopping for people to come over and buy lemonade.

What's the matter with these peo-ple? I crabbed to myself. *Don't they ap-preciate adorable children when they see them doing adorable things like having a lemonade stand?*

Finally a car did pull up, and three men got out. They were wearing army uniforms. I thought they might tell us to get off their armory, but they just smiled at us and two of them walked past, toward the armory.

The third one was the friendliest looking. He came over to the stand.

"How about a glass of nice cold lemonade?" I smiled my best smile.

"Are you crazy? It's forty degrees out here. With a raw wind."

"But how do you expect little kids to earn money if nobody buys their lemonade?"

"That's your problem, kid. If you had any sense, you'd be selling hot drinks on a day like today. Well, I'd better go inside. I'm driving the tank in the Vet's Day parade this afternoon. Have to get it shined up and ready to go."

Kimberley was butterflying all around him. He had to brush her aside and step over Derek to get across the lawn to the armory.

I pouted a while and thought dark thoughts about grown-ups who won't even spend thirty cents to make three children happy.

But then I got to thinking about what he said. If I were selling hot lemonade instead of cold . . .

And that's when the second part of the Plan was born.

☺

I left Kimberley in charge and ran back home for more supplies. *What doesn't burn?* I asked myself as I ran. *Metal,* myself answered.

My executive-steel-trap mind was in full swing now, and I loved it. Cookie sheet. Four great big family-sized cans of baked beans. Matches and newspapers.

"Make some more letters," I commanded Kimberley. It's hard to command and puff at the same time. "Make

H,O,T, and hang them up on top of
LEMONADE. Derek, give me a paw
here."

He had trouble seeing because his
bent-over ears were now hanging in
front of his face, but he tried. We slid
the tub of lemonade to the end of the
dressing table, and I went to work on
my fireplace.

"Derek, fish out those ice cubes," I
told him. "No, not with your woolly
paws, stupid."

He started crying again.

I tried to ignore him. It was easy
because I was having troubles of my
own. I put the cookie sheet on the middle of the dressing table and stood the
four bean cans at each corner of it. But
the dressing table was slanting a little
bit, so things weren't staying where
they were supposed to.

It took all three of us to lift the tub
of lemonade onto the cans and get it to
stay there. Then I remembered the la-
bels on the cans, and I had to go around

peeling them off with my fingernails so they wouldn't catch on fire.

"Okay, here we go," I said. I wadded up a sheet of newspaper, stuck it under the tub, and lit a match.

Derek backed away. "I'm not supposed to play with matches," he said in his good-boy voice.

"Well neither am I," I snapped. "And this is not playing. This is a business enterprise. It's not playing."

Kimberley frowned. "Don't burn my table."

"That's what the cookie sheet is for, dummy." I was getting tired of these assistants.

Kimberley got cold standing around watching, so she started twirling and flapping her arms up and down the sidewalk again while we waited for the lemonade to warm up.

Derek went back to his flat-back somersaults, and I looked hopefully at the cars going by. Since hardly anybody had walked by on the sidewalk the whole time we'd been there, the cars looked like our best bet.

Most of the cars didn't slow down, so when one of them pulled up and stopped, I got excited. A boy rolled down his window and pointed at Kimberley.

"Look, Mommy, that girl is wearing her underwear outside. How come you won't let me wear my underwear in the yard?"

Kimberley stopped dancing and looked murder at him. "It's a dance costume, you idiot," she yelled.

"Want some hot lemonade?" I asked hopefully. But he rolled up the window and they drove on.

"Wearing underwear!" Kimberley screeched at me, like it was my fault. "Anybody who can't tell a butterfly from underwear . . . Derek, quit doing those stupid somersaults. I'm not picking you up anymore. I'm going home. And I want my dressing table back. This was a stupid idea, Zelda."

It wasn't the idea that was stupid,

it was the assistants. I stood with my finger in the lemonade so I could feel it getting warmer.

All of a sudden the wind blew, the dressing table raised its skirt, and one of the sign pages blew back into my fireplace under the tub. The sign caught fire. The skirt started to smoke.

The fire got very hot very fast. I wanted to dump the lemonade on it to put it out but I was scared to get that close.

Suddenly there was a huge *bang! !* Three more—*bang! bang! bang!*

I was blind!

No, I wasn't. I was just covered with baked beans. The cans had exploded.

There was a lot of smoke all around, and a terrible smell. Melting plastic tub, I figured.

Derek was screaming for his mother. Kimberley flapped around the fire, waving her arms for real. She made the fire worse by fanning it.

I danced from one foot to the other.

Should I run and get help? Was it going to burn down the whole block, the trees, the armory, the trailer park? The whole city?

I was so scared I couldn't do anything but jump back and forth from foot to foot.

All of a sudden there were sirens, and a beautiful, wonderful red fire truck came wheeling around the corner and into the armory driveway.

Men jumped off while it was still rolling, and they started pulling down hoses and hatchets. Then they slowed down and just sort of stood looking.

"Hey, move it," somebody bellowed. I looked around. The army tank was coasting down the driveway with the three army guys hanging out from under its lid, waving at us.

"Get the fire truck out of the way. We have to get downtown to the parade. What's on fire? What the . . ."

They stopped their tank and stared at the mess.

Kimberley drooped her wings and stared at the mess.

Derek Rabbit tripped over his feet and started crying again.

The fire was out by then. The dressing table had burned all the way through its middle. It had fallen in a heap along with the exploded bean cans, the twisted cookie sheet, and the green tub with the hole melted through its bottom. And the entire mess was plastered with exploded baked beans and dripped with sticky lemonade.

Actually we had a nice-sized crowd by that time. All the people who hadn't walked past when we wanted them to were there now.

If I'd only had some hot lemonade left to sell them . . .

And then the police car got there, and two familiar-looking policemen got out.

One said, "What's the trouble here?"

The other one looked at me and

said, "Sarge, it's that little girl again."

And then, of course, Mom drove up.

⟲

"You are in huge trouble this time, Zelda Marie. I'm talking mountain-sized trouble. Do you have any idea how dangerous that was? Do you realize you might have gotten burned to death? Do you see why I have told you and *told* you not to play with matches? Do you have any idea what you have done to my blood pressure?"

That was too many questions, so I didn't try to answer any of them. I let her wash the beans off of my face and arms even though I could have done it myself. I figured that as long as she was washing me, she wasn't spanking me.

But she did shove my head under the faucet to wash the beans out of my hair so hard that I wondered if she was trying for a drowning or maybe a broken neck.

"It was for a good cause," I said

humbly. "I was just trying to earn money for your Christmas present."

"I don't give a fat rat *what* you were doing it for. You are never never *never* going to do anything like that, ever again," she bellowed, as she hauled my head out of the sink by the ear.

"I won't," I said from under the towel. I almost lost a nose the way she was rubbing.

"I'm going to have to pay Kimberley's parents for the dressing table and get a new plastic tub to soak my feet in . . ." She ran out of breath.

"And four cans of beans and a cookie sheet," I said in my sorriest voice. "But don't worry, Mom, I'll pay you back. I'll think of some way of earning the money. Maybe I could bake cookies and sell them door to door, or . . ."

The towel got jammed in my mouth.

ᔔ

So that was why this wasn't one of my better Saturdays. After Mom simmered down, we talked about the problem of having my own money to buy her a Christmas present. She said she would much rather have some simple thing that I made by myself in school. Like my handprint in clay, or a pencil holder made out of popsicle sticks glued to a tin can.

It sounded awfully dull to me, but if that's what she wants . . .

5. Zelda, Come Home

It was all Derek's fault. I wouldn't have gotten into all this trouble if it hadn't been for him.

Mom said she would take care of Derek for a few days because his mom and dad wanted to go on a second honeymoon to Railroad World, and they couldn't afford a sitter for him. Mom even took time off from work just for Derek. It was summer, so we didn't have school, and Mom didn't want to dump Derek on Mrs. Birdsall.

So there was Mom, taking vacation days off from work, just to sit around

watching Derek. She wouldn't do that
for me. And Derek's only a little first-
grader, and he's not even her own kid.
That made me a little bit mad to start
with.

Another thing that made me mad
was that whenever Derek did anything
wrong, it was me who got scolded. I
drew a very nice picture, and stupid
Derek folded it over and cut it up in the
shape of a tree. Of course I got mad and
yelled at him, and Mom bawled me out
for yelling. When I told her what he did,
she bawled me out for tattling. I couldn't
win!

"He's our guest," she kept telling
me. But he wasn't a guest, he was just
Derek.

"Be nice to him," Mom told me. So
I tried. I sat him down and showed him
how to shoot rubber bands with his finger, but he couldn't do it. He kept curl-
ing up his hand, and you can't shoot
with a curled up hand. Everybody
knows that. You have to hold your gun

finger out straight, and stick your thumb up. You hook the rubber band over the tip of your little finger, loop it around behind your thumb, and hook the other end over the tip of your gun finger. Then, when you let go with your little finger, it shoots.

But Derek kept dropping his thumb and letting his gun finger curl up so that his rubber band just fell off instead of shooting.

And then he got in my line of fire when I was aiming at the lamp shade, and he got a rubber band in the cheek, and he started crying like I'd done something to him. A rubber band is no big deal. You can shoot it right on yourself and it doesn't hurt. I knew he was crying just to get me in trouble with Mom. He really knows how to use that crying stuff.

It was bad enough having to live with Derek in the way all the time, but the worst was Mom always taking his side. I didn't care if he *was* our guest.

I was her *kid*. I was supposed to be more important to her than anybody. And here she was bawling me out for stuff Derek was doing. As if it was my fault Derek stuck his big head between my shooting finger and my lamp target! I got so mad that I went in my room and slammed the door.

I started trying to figure out ways to get even with him and make Mom love me again. I thought about getting hurt, but that might be painful. I thought about getting sick, but you can't just do that whenever you want to. And Mom can always tell if I pretend I'm sick when I'm not. I've tried that enough to know it never works.

That left only one thing. The Big R.

As soon as I thought of it, I knew I was going to do it. Run away from home. In stories, it always works. The little kid wraps up his belongings in a bandana, ties it on a stick over his shoulder, and runs away from home. But he never gets very far because his mom finds out he's gone, comes after him before he even gets to the corner, and tells him she loves him. Then he gets taken home and fed a big meal and ice cream, and everybody makes a big deal out of it.

Sounded pretty good to me.

The first thing I had to decide was where to run away to. I figured that as long as I was going, I might as well go someplace really good. Disney World sounded about right.

I got down my quarter bank and shook it. It was pretty heavy. I guessed it had about ten or eleven dollars in it. I wasn't sure where Disney World was, but I figured ten dollars would get me started in the right direction anyway.

The next problem was what to take. I didn't have a bandana to wrap my belongings in like you're supposed to when you run away, so I took the pillowcase off my pillow and used that.

I packed my quarter bank, which

was in the shape of the Statue of Liberty. I threw in my sweatshirt with the pink pigs in ballet costumes dancing across it, and my cowboy boots. It was hard to know how much to take. If Mom caught up with me in time, I wouldn't need any of this stuff. If she didn't catch up with me and I got all the way to Disney World, I wasn't going to want to have to carry a lot of heavy stuff.

Besides, I thought, *if I go walking around town looking like a kid running away from home, I might get picked up by somebody who'll bring me back. And if I'm brought back before Mom has a chance to learn her lesson, it won't do any good.*

Cagey, I told myself. *Be cagey about this, Zelda. Travel light. Act like a grown-up, and maybe nobody will catch you.*

So I dumped out the pillowcase and got ready to travel light. I put on the pink pigs sweatshirt even though it was hot outside. I was going to need those good old pigs of mine for company, in case things got scary out there.

I put my Statue of Liberty bank up under my sweatshirt, and stuck the bottom of it in my shorts so it wouldn't fall out. I put on my favorite sandals.

Then for the important part. I got out a sheet of notebook paper and wrote the note. You always have to write a note when you do the Big R. Otherwise they won't know where to come looking for you.

"Dear Mom. You don't love me anymore because you'd rather have Derek. So I'm running away from home. I'm going to Disney World, so don't try to find me. Your former daughter, Zelda Marie Hammersmith."

I left it on my pillow. Then I took it off again and made my bed so the note would be sure to show up, and I set it against the pillow again.

Mom was in the living room watching cartoons on television. With Derek in her lap. It was sickening.

I said, "Goodbye forever, Mother."

She said, "Come and watch 'Roadrunner' with us."

"I can't. I'm running away from home."

"Ho-ho," she said.

I slammed out the door. I'd give her something to ho-ho about.

↻

There was a place a few blocks from our trailer park where two or three taxicabs were usually parked. I decided that would be the way to go, since I wasn't sure where Disney World was. I'd never ridden in a cab before, but I knew from watching television that all you have to do is get in and tell the driver where you want to go, and he takes you there.

So I did it. I walked up to the first cab and got in the back seat. The driver turned around and looked at me. He was a great big man with cheeks that sagged clear down to his collar.

"Get outa my cab, kid. This ain't no playground."

I stuck my nose in the air. "I am a customer. I want you to take me to Disney World."

"What?"

"I'm going to Disney World," I said, louder, in case he was hard of hearing. I wondered if Mom had read my note yet. I looked out the window, but I couldn't see her anywhere.

"Are you serious? A little kid like you, going all the way to Florida by yourself? Come on, pull my other leg. It's got bells on."

Florida. That was a long way away. I'd have to fly, to get all the way to Florida. That was probably going to cost a lot more than I had. *Oh well*, I thought. *One problem at a time.*

"Take me to the airport," I said in a very grown-up voice.

He frowned at me. "Are you sure you're supposed to be running around alone? You look awful young to me. Does your mother know where you are?"

That was a silly question. What kid, in the middle of doing the Big R, is going to admit it?

"I'm meeting my mother at the airport," I said. "Now step on it."

He started the cab. "You got money?" he asked darkly.

"Of course."

We drove and drove and *drove*. I didn't think we were ever going to get there. But finally I saw a lot of big planes coming right down, practically over the cab. We stopped by a curb, and the driver came around to help me out. "Eleven dollars," he said.

"What?"

"That's the fare, kid. You owe me eleven dollars. Plus tip."

I stared at him. That was all my money. Maybe even more than all my money. Just for a car ride. But he was an awfully big man, and he towered over me looking like the giant in "Jack and the Beanstalk." So I sat down on the curb and started shaking quarters out of the Statue of Liberty.

"Come on, come on. I haven't got all day," the driver said.

"Dollar fifty, dollar seventy-five . . ."

People were walking by and giving me funny looks, but I kept on shaking and counting. "Four twenty-five, four fifty . . ."

"Are you going to pay an eleven dollar fare all in quarters?" the driver bellowed. "Now I remember why I never got married and had kids."

"Well you would have been an awfully crabby father, if you did," I snapped back. "Seven. Seven twenty-five . . ."

The total came out eleven dollars and one quarter. I gave him the extra quarter for his tip, but he was still muttering darkly when he drove away.

I stuck the Statue of Liberty back up under my shirt and started through

the big doors into the airport. I reached
to push the door open, but it jumped
back when it saw me coming, just like
the door at the Super-Valu. I would like
to have stayed and jumped on and off
the mat a few times, but I had more
important things to do.

The airport was the hugest place I
had ever been in. I couldn't even see the
ends of it anywhere. People were walking and running back and forth, swerv-
ing around me, pulling little carts full
of suitcases. It was part scary and part
exciting.

I saw a counter that said *Information,* so I asked the lady where I could
get the plane to Disney World. At first
she couldn't see me because the counter
was too high. I had to take out my
Statue of Liberty and wave it back and
forth to get her attention.

"Disney World," she said in a bored
voice. "That would be Orlando. Check
with the TWA counter."

I didn't know what a Twa counter was, or why she had to spell it when it wasn't even a bad word, but she didn't look like she was going to tell me any more, so I started looking around.

All along the back row of this endless room, were counters with different signs up over them: Air Midwest, and United, and—yes—there it was. Twa.

I went over to the Twa counter and stood around for a long time. I wanted to ask where the plane was that was going to Orlando, but everyone there was too busy talking to people with suitcases. So I decided to explore on my own.

Outside a big window I could see some airplanes, so I headed that way down the hallway. I wasn't sure how I was going to get on the plane if I did find it. I didn't have any money left to buy a ticket after that cab guy got through with me. But I figured something would turn up.

I followed some Twa signs into another hallway. I started to go down it, but a woman in a blue uniform stopped me.

"You have to go through security," she said.

I wasn't sure what that meant, so I just stood back and watched other people do it for a while. It was a funny-looking place. There was a counter that moved, like at the Super-Valu. But instead of putting groceries on it, you had to put your purse or your bags or whatever you were carrying. Then the purses all disappeared behind a black curtain. They came out again on the other end of the counter, but I didn't trust that counter one little bit. Even if there wasn't any money in my statue any more, I sure wasn't going to put it on that counter.

Beside the counter was a thing like a telephone booth with no front or back. People walked through it after they put their bags on the moving counter. Then after they walked through it, they could get their purses back.

I wondered if they shot you with rays when you walked through.

On the wall was a big sign telling you not to make jokes about security. I wasn't going to until I read the sign. Then I started feeling like I would explode if I couldn't make a joke. Like when someone tells you not to smile, and then you can't help it.

There were three not-smiling women in uniforms working around the moving counter. They were watching people as they walked through the phone booth. They had eagle eyes, and they weren't letting anybody get past them without going through the booth. And the only way you could get to the airplanes was through the booth and past those three not-smiling women.

I sucked in a big breath and marched forward.

૭

I took one last look all around, to see if Mom was coming. She wasn't. Casually I stepped into the booth.

Bells rang. Red lights flashed. I stopped dead in my tracks. I looked around to see what it was.

It was *me*.

All three of the uniformed women turned on me.

"You have metal on you," the closest one said. "Step over here, please, and empty your pockets."

Metal? Then I realized what all this security stuff was about. They were checking people for bombs. So no one could bomb an airplane, like on television.

Well, the only metal I had was my Statue of Liberty quarter bank, and they sure weren't getting that away from me. It was bad enough having to give that cab driver all the quarters out of it. I was still mad about that.

"Empty your pockets please," another security woman said. She said it in a nicer voice, like she knew I wasn't a mad bomber. But I didn't have any pockets and I didn't want them to get my bank. I got scared all of a sudden. *Mom, where are you when I need you?*

I cut and ran. Around the security women, down the long wide crowded hallway, toward the airplanes. If I could find one going to Disney World, and figure out a way to get on it . . .

Or if Mom would hurry up and get here, and get me out of this mess. I didn't know which way I wanted to go, to Orlando or to Mom. I just knew people were chasing me, and I had to run.

I could have run a lot faster than the security women. I could have dodged around people quicker than they could. Except. Except my sandals kept almost slipping off, and I had to curl up my toes to hold them on. Then the Statue of Liberty started slipping down into my shorts, and I had to grab it with one hand.

I was still in the Twa department.

On either side of the wide hallway were big living rooms with rows of black leather chairs full of people waiting to get on planes. Out the window I could see planes parked up close so I figured I was getting warmer. If I could just slow down long enough to ask one of the Twa people, I could probably find my plane.

But the security people were gaining on me from behind. All of a sudden there were two of them in front of me. Men, this time. I saw a sign right over my head that said Rest Room.

Quickly I ran inside. I figured the security men couldn't follow me in there.

Wrong! I slid to a fast stop and looked around. This wasn't the Ladies' Room. There were men in it! They turned from washing their hands to stare at me.

"Oops," I said, turning around.

The security men caught me on the rebound. They held my elbows and said, "Hold on there, little lady."

I stopped dead still, and the Statue of Liberty dropped out of my shorts and went *clank* on the floor.

One of the men picked it up. The security women caught up, panting and grabbing their sides. The man held up my quarter bank, shook it, looked at it, and looked at the women. They looked at me.

"It's a kid's piggy bank," he said, disgusted.

"No," I said. "That's the Statue of Liberty. See? She's holding up her flashlight, and she's got the spikes coming out of her head and everything. That's the Stat . . ."

"You mean," he said to the women, "you rang the alarm and had half the force out here chasing a little kid with a piggy bank?"

"No," I said again. "It's not a pig, it's the . . ."

One of the women said, "Well she set off the scanner, and when we asked her to empty her pockets, she ran. You know what the rules are. No exceptions, not even for . . ." She looked down at me like I was a worm. "Not even for little kids with piggy banks."

"No," I said again. I was getting tired of explaining this. "It's the Statue of Liberty. See? And she's holding up her . . ."

"Oh, get out of here," the man said.

I guessed that meant I wasn't under arrest anymore.

I took off down the hall, then stopped to talk to a Twa man who was standing behind a tall table at the entrance to one of the living rooms. "Where is the plane to Orlando?"

"Flight three thirty-eight, gate twenty-one, now boarding," he said.

Gate twenty-one was right across the hall. I looked up and down for Mom, but still no luck. It was sure taking her a long time to find me. *Maybe she isn't trying all that hard,* I thought. *Maybe she figures Derek is less trouble than I am. Maybe she's enjoying being rid of me.*

I wanted to sit down somewhere and cry a while, but I figured I'd have time to do that once I got on my plane.

There was a long line of people going from the gate twenty-one living room into a long tunnel. They were going past another Twa man who was standing in the tunnel doorway looking at their tickets.

I didn't have a ticket. I didn't have money to buy one. I was about to panic and give up when I saw what I needed.

A fat man.

He was a really fat man, not just jolly and plump. He was very tall and very fat. He was perfect.

I eased up beside him and a little bit behind, so that he didn't notice me. The woman behind us gave me a dirty look for crowding, but that couldn't be helped.

Closer and closer to the Twa man

we went. Closer and closer to my shield
I edged. He held out his ticket. I shrank
myself up as much as I could and hid
behind that beautiful big stomach.

As we passed the Twa man I eased
forward, keeping the fat man between
me and the Twa guy. Then we were past
and into the tunnel. I ran ahead, down
a long sloping alley of green carpet that
turned a corner and became the inside
of an airplane.

Wow.

I slowed down and fell in behind a
man and woman, like I was with them,
and smiled when the Twa lady welcomed us aboard.

The aisle down the middle of the
plane was very skinny, and it was full
of people putting bags on shelves over
their heads. I got tired of standing and
waiting for Mom, so I sat down in a seat
by the window.

If Mom was going to come after me,
she didn't have much time. Otherwise
I was on my way to Disney World. I tried

to get back my excitement about that, but all I could think was that Mom didn't come after me.

Well, if she didn't want me, then I didn't want her, either. I would just go stay in Disney World forever. But somehow, I wasn't very happy about that.

I sniffed and started to bawl.

ᘒ

Before I could get wound up for a really good cry, a man's voice above me said, "Excuse me. You're in my seat."

"What?"

"Six A," he said. "That's my seat."

I got out and worked my way back through the crowd and sat in another empty seat.

Another man came along and said it was his. I was getting a little tired of this. But since I didn't want to draw attention to myself and get thrown off, I politely got up and moved to *another* seat, way at the back this time.

"That's my seat."

I sighed and looked up. At least this one was younger. He looked more like a teenager than a man, and he was holding a guitar case. He shoved the guitar into the shelf over our heads, and then he stood aside to let me out.

"Nuts to this," I said. "Two other guys came along and made me get out of my seat, and now you're the third one. Finders keepers. I found this seat. Now you go find one of your own."

"Look, twerp," he said in a nasty voice, "Twenty-three A. That's my seat. It's right here on my ticket. Let's see your ticket. It'll have your seat number on it."

I got red in the face.

A lady in the seat ahead turned around and said, "What's the matter, honey. Can't you find your seat? Let's see your ticket. I'll help you."

Think fast, I told myself. But I never can when I have to. "I lost it." It was the best I could come up with.

From across the aisle a man said,

"Are you traveling with a parent or guardian?"

They always say that at school: parent or guardian. You have to have things signed by your parent or guardian. I always think of a guardian angel when they say that. One of those would certainly come in handy about now.

"No," I told him in a grown-up voice. "I'm traveling alone."

"Oh," he said. "Stewardess. Stewardess! Here's a child traveling alone."

I looked at him, feeling guilty. Was a child traveling alone against the rules, too, like not emptying your pockets at the security place?

A Twa lady appeared and said, "I don't have you on my list, dear. They always alert us when a child is traveling alone. What's your name and seat number?"

I couldn't think of a thing to say. I couldn't even remember my name.

"Let me see your ticket," she said in a gentle voice.

I just looked at her. From a couple of rows ahead, my fat man said, "Hah. She's probably a stowaway. Come to think of it, I believe I saw her slip past the ticket taker. Figured she was with the woman behind me."

A woman's voice piped up. "I thought she was with you."

"No, she wasn't with me. I thought she was with you."

The Twa lady squatted down to my level and said, "Honey, did you have a ticket?"

I shook my head.

"Well, you know you can't ride without a ticket. Where is your mother or father?"

"My dad is in Nashville trying to be a country and western star," I said.

People giggled.

I glared at them and said, "My mom is home. She could have come after me, but she didn't. She's got Derek now, and he's not as much trouble as I am."

The boy with the guitar said,

"You're running away from home. Right on, sister. I ran away, too, when I was sixteen. So who is your dad? Would I know him? I've played a few gigs in Nashville. What is he—singer, banjo, guitar, or what?"

"He mostly sings," I told him. "He sends Mom and me pictures of him singing and playing his guitar. That's how I knew you had a guitar in that case. His is bright red, with little shooting stars all over it. What color is yours?"

"The kid is running away from home on a jet," the man across the aisle said. "What ever happened to the good old days when kids ran away from home on foot? Why, back in my day . . ."

"The poor little thing," said the woman in front of me. "I think you should let her ride free. It's a big airline. You can afford it."

The fat man said, "Throw the kid off. That's the way juvenile delinquents get started. People give in to them. I'm paying two hundred and eighty-five dollars for this flight. She should have to, too."

Two hundred and eighty-five dollars! Wow. Plane tickets cost more than a pony.

The man across the aisle said, "Get the kid out of here so we can take off. I have to meet a connecting flight in St. Louis."

The woman in front said, "Listen, she can sit on my lap if you don't have any empty seats. In fact, she can stay with me at my daughter's house. She's more interesting than my grandchildren. All they do is sit on their fannies and play video games. You want to go to Disney World with me, honey? My grandkids have seen it so often they never want to go with me when I visit."

"Yeah," I said, brightening.

"No," yelled the fat man. "You can't let her ride free. I'll complain to the airlines. I'll complain to the FAA. I'll complain . . ."

Another Twa man appeared over the heads around me. He was the handsomest man I'd ever seen in my life. Right away, while I was falling in love with him, I knew he was the captain. Pilot. Whatever they call the head guy.

"What's the trouble here," he said in a beautiful, low, singing voice.

The stewardess stood up and explained. The gorgeous hunk smiled down on me and said, "Sorry, sweetheart, we'll have to deplane you."

I figured that meant kick me off.

"Aw," said the guitar guy, "come on. Let the kid ride. You only run away from home once. Let her do it in style. I had to hitchhike across Oklahoma in August."

The woman in front stood up and said, "Attention, everyone, we're going to take a vote. All in favor of letting this little girl stay on board, raise your right hand."

No one raised their right hand.

Sighing, I stood up. "Thanks any-way," I told her.

The man of my dreams picked me up and carried me off the plane. The thrill of that was almost worth the trouble. Over his shoulder I waved goodbye, and everyone waved back.

Even the fat man.

☺

They put me in the security people's room where they could watch me while they called Mom to come and get me.

It took her a long time to get there. In fact I was wondering if she was even going to come. I was pretty sure she would, but I was even more sure she was going to be awfully mad at me.

And she was. She hugged me a lot, and cried, and yelled at me for scaring her out of ten years' growth, whatever that meant.

"How could you do such a thing, Zelda Marie Hammersmith? I was going out of my mind trying to find you."

"Did you really try to find me?" I brightened up a little.

"Of course I did, pea-brain. You disappear without a word, you're gone for hours, and I have no idea where you are or what might have happened to you."

"Well, I *told* you I was running away from home," I said.

She looked blank.

"When you were watching 'Roadrunner' and holding stupid Derek on your lap," I explained. "I stood right there and told you I was running away from home, and you just said 'ho-ho.'"

"I didn't take you seriously," she yelled. "No kid stands there and says she's running away from home. If she really means it, she sneaks out. If you'd snuck out I'd have believed you."

I dropped my head and stuck out my lip. "I left you a note on my bed. That's what you're supposed to do when you run away. I left you a perfectly good note, and I told you I was going to Disney World. But you didn't come after me like you were supposed to."

She stopped and thought. "Oh. Derek was cutting trees out of a piece of paper he found in your room. That was probably it."

"You let Derek cut trees out of my running-away note? You never let me cut up good stuff."

Then she looked at me hard. "Aha. That's what all this is about. You're jealous of Derek. Zelda, you've done some really pea-brained things in your day, and this is one of them. You've got nobody to be jealous of, not Derek or anybody else."

"I don't?"

"No. Derek is a nice little neighbor boy whom I'm taking care of for a few days. You are the heart in the big middle of my life. You know that."

I dropped my head farther down and looked up at her. "You haven't told me that for a long time."

"I'm telling you now," she said

firmly, and she stood up. "Let's get out of here. I had to leave Derek with Mrs. Birdsall, and I don't think she can take too much of him."

We walked down the long hallway toward the airport door, holding hands.

"Why can't she stand him, Mom?"

She gave my hand a squeeze. "Oh, he's a nice enough little boy, but he is kind of boring. Compared to you."